As the door closed, the room fell silent. Just like that, they were alone.

His heart was suddenly hammering inside his chest. So, this was it. He had imagined this moment so many times inside his head. Had thought of all the clever, caustic things to say, only now his mind was blank.

Not that it mattered, he thought, anger pulsing over his skin. Sooner or later, she was going to realize that he wasn't going to disappear this time.

Not until he'd got what he came for.

Her eyes locked with his. He felt his heart tighten around the shard of ice that had been lodged there ever since Dove had cast him into the wilderness.

She was staring at him in silence, and he waited just as he had waited in that hotel bar. Only this time, she was the one who didn't know what was happening. Didn't know that she was about to be chewed up and spat out. But she would, soon enough.

"What are you doing here, Gabriel?" Her voice was husky but it was hearing her say his name again that made his breathing jerk.

Louise Fuller was a tomboy who hated pink and always wanted to be the prince—not the princess! Now she enjoys creating heroines who aren't pretty pushovers but are strong, believable women. Before writing for Harlequin, she studied literature and philosophy at university, then worked as a reporter on her local newspaper. She lives in Royal Tunbridge Wells with her impossibly handsome husband, Patrick, and their six children.

Books by Louise Fuller

Harlequin Presents

The Man She Should Have Married
Italian's Scandalous Marriage Plan
Beauty in the Billionaire's Bed
The Italian's Runaway Cinderella
Maid for the Greek's Ring
Their Dubai Marriage Makeover

Christmas with a Billionaire

The Christmas She Married the Playboy

Visit the Author Profile page
at Harlequin.com for more titles.

Louise Fuller

RETURNING FOR HIS RUTHLESS REVENGE

HARLEQUIN

PRESENTS

Recycling programs
for this product may
not exist in your area.

ISBN-13: 978-1-335-73923-0

Returning for His Ruthless Revenge

Copyright © 2023 by Louise Fuller

For questions and comments about the quality of this book,
please contact us at CustomerService@Harlequin.com.

Harlequin Enterprises ULC
22 Adelaide St. West, 41st Floor
Toronto, Ontario M5H 4E3, Canada
www.Harlequin.com

Printed in U.S.A.

RETURNING FOR HIS RUTHLESS REVENGE

Thanks to Vic and Awo. If you hadn't stuck with me on the last book, I would never have gotten to write this one.

CHAPTER ONE

'GOOD MORNING, MS CAVENDISH. Did you have a good holiday?'

Without breaking her stride, Dove Cavendish turned towards the young paralegal who had interrupted her thoughts and her progress across the foyer of Cavendish and Cox and forced her lips into the shape of a small, careless smile.

'I did, yes. Thank you, Mollie.'

'You picked a good week to take off. There was another tube strike on Wednesday and loads of us didn't get into work until halfway through the morning.' Mollie hesitated. 'Oh, and we've got a new client. Did you hear? I mean, about Mr—?'

Before she could say his name, Dove cut her off with a swift, emphatic nod. 'I did, yes,' she repeated. It was all her numb mind could come up with.

A shiver ran down her spine and her cheeks felt hot, but she knew her expression would not betray her. Growing up as the Band-Aid baby of her parents' failing marriage, she had learned early on to keep her thoughts to herself and concentrate on defusing conflict. It was one of the reasons she was so good at her job as a corporate lawyer. Even today, when her carefully rebuilt world had been knocked off its orbit, nobody would ever guess what she was really thinking. What she had been thinking since her boss, Alistair Cox, had called her at home last night.

She had just returned from a long overdue and much-needed week away, and had been in the middle of emptying her bag. It hadn't been a long conversation, and truthfully she'd barely heard most of what Alistair had been saying, but after he'd hung up she hadn't had the strength to finish unpacking. This morning her suitcase was still on the floor in her bedroom, gaping open as if, like her, it was still in shock at his bombshell revelation.

Gabriel Silva had hired Cavendish and Cox to handle his latest acquisition. M&A.

She stopped in front of the lift.

Gabriel Silva.

The name pulsed inside her head in time with her heartbeat as she watched the numbers light up.

At thirty years old, he was a legend in the corporate world—an apex predator in an ocean filled with hunters…killers. Ruthless, relentless, never tiring, he pursued his prey remorselessly and in doing so had built one of the most successful businesses in the world from scratch.

But it wasn't his business reputation that was making a silent scream of panic rise up inside her.

Six years ago, Gabriel Silva had broken off their relationship and broken her heart. Actually, he had shattered it into a thousand pieces. And he hadn't simply broken up with her. Her father, Oscar, had offered him money to disappear from her life and Gabriel had accepted his offer, pocketing the cash and walking away without so much as a word of explanation or apology.

And now he was back.

Her throat tightened. People said that time was a great healer: they were wrong. Hearing Alistair say his name last night had been like a serrated blade slicing through her skin. The pain of his rejection was as raw and as agonising just as if it had happened yesterday.

'It's pretty exciting, isn't it?' Mollie looked over at her, her brown eyes wide with undisguised awe. 'I Googled him this morning and he's like the real deal.'

No, he isn't, Dove thought, her heart lurching forward as the lift doors opened. There was nothing real about Gabriel Silva.

Everything—every word, every smile, every touch—had been fake. All of it carefully staged to look like the real thing so that she would take the bait. And she had. Despite knowing that 'love' was a hoax, a bow to prettify something essentially pragmatic and transactional, she had allowed herself to be reeled in.

And, like every other gullible woman who had

fallen for a pair of blue eyes and a brain-melting smile, she had paid the price. Or rather her father had. And that hurt the most. Not just that Gabriel had never loved her, but that her love for him had been transformed into currency in some horrible, distorted alchemy.

There was only one positive in the whole sorry mess. Knowing how everyone would react to her dating a man whose father was an electrician, she and Gabriel had kept their relationship secret. No one other than her father had known the truth, and Oscar had died a month after Gabriel left—not of a broken heart but a diseased one. So her humiliation had been hers alone.

As much as she'd wanted to confide in her mother, she hadn't. Not when she'd known how devastated Olivia would be.

She knew the story of her parents' marriage back to front and inside out. Officially, it had been the love story of their generation. Beautiful, wealthy American heiress Olivia Morgan and handsome, upperclass Englishman Oscar Cavendish.

But just weeks after exchanging their vows the marriage had been floundering. The bills for Oscar's expensive tastes—including her mother's engagement ring and the honeymoon—had started rolling in. Only Oscar had had no money to pay them. His inheritance was gone, and he'd had no intention of doing anything as menial as working.

It had been the start of a very long and disappointing marriage, and ever since Dove could remember her mother had warned her daughters—particularly her youngest—against making the same mistake. Or maybe it just felt that way because she was the last one at home and there was nobody around to dilute Olivia's fears.

Either way, given her mother's feelings about men without money but with ulterior motives, she had never been able to bear to tell her the truth.

Diverting her thoughts away from that particularly unedifying dead end, Dove leaned back against the wall of the lift as it started to move upwards jerkily. Like everything else in the firm's Grade II listed headquarters in Lincoln's Inn Fields, it needed upgrading, but clients didn't come to Cavendish and Cox for glossy interiors. They came because they wanted a lawyer they could trust implicitly—they came for Alistair Cox.

Her pulse darted. Or that was what they usually came for anyway. But was the same true of Gabriel Silva?

Feeling Mollie's gaze on her face, she blanked her mind to all the possible and equally unnerving answers to Mollie's observation. 'Yes, he is the real deal,' she agreed. 'But I shouldn't get too excited, Mollie. It will be Mr Silva's people we'll be dealing with. Not the man himself.'

Of that she was certain. He would review the data as it was presented to him, and obviously it would be his signature on the dotted line, but he wouldn't be a part of the exhaustive day-to-day process of negotiation and due diligence.

'But *he* must have had the final say.' Mollie smiled up at her shyly. 'Which means we must be the best. Why else would he hire us?'

That question again. Her stomach lurched. *Were* Cavendish and Cox the best? Historically, yes. Nowadays they had rivals for the top spot, but their name still carried weight. Then again, they were a small family firm. Too small and traditional to be a natural fit for a slick, carnivorous outfit like the Silva Group.

A natural fit.

Her stomach did a slow somersault as her brain unhelpfully offered up a memory of Gabriel's sunsoaked body moving against hers. They had fitted together like pieces of a puzzle, their hot, damp skin sticking, his hand splayed against her back, her breath scratching in her throat as their bodies arched into one another—

'I'm afraid that's not something you or I can really answer,' Dove said, feeling a rush of relief as the lift shuddered to a halt. Have a good day, Mollie.'

'Ah good—there you are. Don't worry, he's only just arrived.'

She blinked. Alistair was standing slightly to the left of the lift, his reading glasses perched precariously on top of his once blond, now grey hair, a clutch of files in his right hand.

'Who's just arrived?'

Her boss frowned. 'Gabriel Silva, of course.'

For some reason, even though her stomach was in freefall, it wasn't hard to smile and say with apparent sincerity, 'That's wonderful.'

Alistair beamed at her. 'Annabel is getting everything set up. I'm going to go down and meet him.'

She nodded, still smiling madly. She felt as if she was outside of her body, watching herself react. Or rather, not react.

'So I'll see you in the war room.'

Dove felt her smile freeze on her face as a ripple of foreboding snaked down her spine. *'Me?'* Her heart was jumping against her ribs like a trapped bird banging into a window. 'Why do I need to be there?'

'Because Mr Silva has specifically asked for you to be at the meeting. I told you last night. Remember? Seems he met your father once, several years ago, and never forgot the encounter.' Alistair paused, pursing his lips, as if he couldn't quite believe what he was about to say. 'They had a good chat, apparently. About his options for the future.' His mild, grey eyes rested on her face. 'I don't know what Oscar said, but it made quite an impression on our Mr Silva. "Life-changing", he called it.'

Her heart was thudding in her throat. That chat hadn't just changed her life, it had destroyed it, and now he was threatening to destroy the fragile life she had rebuilt.

So tell him. Tell Alistair you can't be in the same room as this man. You're like a daughter to him. He won't make you do it.

But it was too late. Her boss was gone. She stared at the lift doors, feeling sick. This couldn't be happening. Except it was. Gabriel Silva was in the building, and any moment now he would be stepping through those doors.

Muscles tensing, she let her eyes flicker down the corridor to the staircase. She could leave—just go now. Walk out of the building and disappear, just like he had done. Only something inside her baulked at the idea. It wouldn't be disappearing—it would be hiding.

And why should she hide? She had done nothing wrong. And besides, she thought, stomach lurching, if she didn't turn up it would look as if she still cared about him, and she couldn't bear for him to think that was true.

Plus, it wouldn't be fair on Alistair to leave him in the lurch. Picturing the look of confusion on her boss's face as he discovered her absence, she snapped her shoulders back.

It would be fine. If Gabriel had wanted to meet her one on one he could easily have arranged to do so. Just because he was curious about the woman he had left behind, it didn't mean it was some kind of reconciliation. It was a business meeting in the war room. First, though, she needed to apply some war paint…

Five minutes later, her cheeks lightly flushed, hair smoothed into a low ponytail, she walked through the door, her pulse twitching a beat behind the click of her heels.

'Here she is.' Alistair greeted her warmly.

His flushed face was comforting and familiar, and just for a moment she kept looking at him, as if by doing so she could somehow ignore the man standing to his right. But even now, even when she hated him with every fibre, she couldn't resist the pull of the past or the demands of the present. And, lifting her chin, she turned to face Gabriel Silva.

Her pulse stumbled, and for a moment she couldn't move—couldn't feel anything. Her body was as rigid and cold as if it had been frozen. And then pain swept through her, scraping against the scars that should have healed but hadn't. A pain that tore at the protective barriers she had built between herself and the world. And she wanted to turn and run and keep running until she found somewhere she could hide away.

After six desolate years, it was a shock to come face to face with him. She had hoped that time might have punished him for what he'd done. But, as her eyes fixed on his absurdly handsome face, she was forced to admit that he was still the most beautiful man she had ever laid eyes on—and the most masculine. Thick dark hair that looked black in the moonlight, a curving, sensual mouth, and those mesmerising, unyielding blue, blue eyes.

Lifting a hand to the single-strand pearl choker at her throat, she breathed in shakily.

And then there was his body—

Her throat was suddenly impossibly dry. She had never seen him in a suit before, and she very much wished she hadn't now. Because she doubted she would ever forget it. There was something about the severity of its cut that softened his fierce beauty and made a knot of something hot and tight pulse in her belly.

Something that should have perished at the same time he turned their 'relationship' into a financial transaction.

Despair and frustration punched her in the gut. She didn't want to feel like this. She shouldn't be feeling like this. Gabriel Silva was a cold-blooded chancer, and the only reason she was even deigning to meet him was Alistair, the man standing beside him.

Stepping forward, Gabriel held out his hand and she stood there, her heart lurching against her ribs. Now, even though it hurt to look at him, it was impossible to turn away.

'Ms Cavendish.'

He was smiling, and suddenly she couldn't seem to breathe, because the Gabriel she had fallen in love with had rarely smiled. When he had it had been miraculous—like the 'fire rainbows' they had seen above Dorset on one of their secret weekends away together. Only this smile was something entirely different. It was calculated, disposable, and purely for Alistair's benefit.

She knew that the moment their gazes met and his eyes slammed into hers with such force that she almost lost her balance.

On the days when she thought she might choke on her sadness she would imagine this moment. Imagine how she would deliver a cool, cutting critique of his character. Instead, she said quietly, 'Mr Silva.'

Reaching out, she took his outstretched hand, intending simply to shake it briefly. But as their palms brushed she felt a jolt of heat, sharp and stinging, like the lick of a flame. His eyes locked with hers and his hand momentarily tightened.

'So this is the family firm,' he said softly, finally loosening his grip. 'Although I understand from Alistair that your father didn't work here?'

'No.' She flexed her fingers, trying to look calm and unaffected. Trying to forget that jolt of heat. Trying not to let her brain linger on how simply shaking hands with him could make her feel so on edge and exposed. 'He thought he lacked the talent for business,' she said stiffly.

In truth, Oscar Cavendish had been smart, and ruthless enough to have reached the top in whatever profession he chose. But he had been lazy and self-indulgent and, unlike Alistair, instead of working at the law firm founded jointly by their great-great-great-grandfathers—or working at all, for that matter—he'd preferred to live off the dividends from his shares in the business.

'And yet he was instrumental in kick-starting *my* career.'

Her heart thudded painfully as he held her gaze.

'Without his input I would never have been able to make that first investment.'

Input.

The word tasted like ash in her mouth. That was one way of describing it. But it was a little opaque, imprecise…misleading, even. Most people—herself and Alistair, for example—would call it a bribe, although no doubt Oscar had called it something less vulgar. An inducement, perhaps. Either way, Gabriel had accepted the money. He had been paid to break her heart.

Are you proud of yourself? Of what you did?

A part of her wanted to beat her fists against his chest and scream bitter, accusatory questions at him. Only that would take them back to the past, and she didn't want to go there. She didn't want to scrape a wound that was still weeping and sore. She just wanted to get this over with, and then get as far away from him as soon as possible.

'Well, thank you for sharing that with me.'

She didn't like the way he was looking at her. It made her feel like a rabbit caught in the headlights of an oncoming car. But this time she wasn't going to let him flatten her.

She had met him, and looked him in the eye, and now she was done.

Straightening her slim shoulders, she lifted her chin. 'I'll let you two get down to business.'

'Of course, of course…' Oblivious to the current of tension swimming around the room, Alistair nodded enthusiastically. 'That's why we're all here.'

Actually, it wasn't, Gabriel thought shifting back in his seat, his lowered gaze fixed on Dove's delicate profile. He was here for one reason and one reason only: revenge. The acquisition of Fairlight Holdings was necessary only to achieve that goal.

The woman standing in front of him also had a part to play. Not that she knew that yet. But no matter. Revenge was a dish best eaten cold, so why not drag things out for just a little longer? Make sure everything was nice and chilled. A couple of minutes would make no difference in the scheme of things. In fact, he was going to enjoy every moment of making her squirm. It was the least she deserved after the way she had treated him.

Remembering the expression on Oscar's smoothly, handsome face as he apologised for his daughter's 'change of heart', he felt his back tensed against the chair.

What heart? Dove Cavendish didn't have one. She was a living, breathing Snow Queen, with ice in her veins, and even now the memory of that conversation with her father burned him—almost as much as her beauty dazzled him.

She was still beautiful.

More than beautiful, he corrected himself reluctantly. She could be a mythical goddess, with her long pale blonde hair and ethereal silvery grey eyes. He had been looking into those same silvery grey eyes when she'd told him she loved him.

Was it any wonder he had been smitten?

He felt something flicker across his skin, and he recognised the hot lick of shame. Later, he had questioned his intelligence and his sanity in believing what Dove had said to him as she lay in his arms. But back then, blinded, foolish, senseless with love, it hadn't been until Oscar Cavendish turned up at the hotel with his 'proposal' that he'd understood how naive, not to say stupid, he had been to think she wanted anything more than a summer fling.

Now, though, it appeared that *she* was the naive one.

Swallowing the bitter taste that rose in the back of his throat, Gabriel turned towards Alistair Cox. 'And I'm very much looking forward to Cavendish and Cox helping me achieve my goal.'

The older man gestured towards the Herman Miller chairs tucked around the large conference table. 'Then let's get started. Thank you, Dove—'

'Oh, Ms Cavendish doesn't need to go.' He glanced over to where Dove stood, poised to leave, her body turned away from him so that he could see the silhouetted curve of her breasts against her blouse. 'We're all friends here.'

Something flashed in those molten silver eyes,

just as they'd used to when they'd made love and he wondered if they still did. And, if so, with whom? His jaw tensed. The thought of another man holding her close at night, touching her, pressing his body against hers, made him see every shade of red.

He steadied his breathing. Once upon a time he'd thought they were friends, lovers. Soulmates, too. Not now. This was not some sort of reconciliation. He didn't want or need to be her friend. In fact, enemies could be just as useful and committed as friends— given the right incentive.

Fortunately, he knew exactly which buttons to press to ensure Dove Cavendish's compliance.

'And besides, my interest in acquiring Fairlight Holdings will soon be made public,' he said softly.

'Fairlight Holdings?' Alistair Cox frowned. 'I knew old Angus Balfour. He made some good investments in the mid-nineties' property rebound, but they made a mistake, in my opinion, when they failed to extend beyond the residential market.'

Gabriel held his gaze. There was a steeliness behind the older man's soft grey eyes, and a first-class brain. Despite his genial demeanour, Alistair Cox was clearly not just some clueless beneficiary playing at the family firm. So how had he ended up getting in such a mess?

Not that it mattered to him. Nothing mattered to him except getting even with the two women who had so callously upended his life. His mother, Fenella Ogilvy, and the woman standing opposite him, who was doing her best to pretend she wasn't there. Or more likely that he wasn't. But this time he wasn't going anywhere. This time he was the one with all the power—and most importantly the money.

Alistair Cox smiled at him pleasantly. 'Which is why I would advise choosing a company with a broader portfolio that covers commercial units as well. I know of a couple that would be interested—'

'Maybe another time,' Gabriel said neutrally.

The older man lifted off his glasses and began polishing them on the cuff of his jumper. 'Might I ask why you're so interested in Fairlight?'

Gabriel stared at Cox impassively, the anger he had held tightly inside for so long tearing at him.

His interest in this acquisition had nothing to do with business. His empire had started just five years ago, with a stake in the social media app Trill, and it had grown, hydra-headed, into a diverse portfolio that included a cryptocurrency exchange, a slow-food restaurant chain, several media outlets, and most recently some commercial real estate in New York.

Unlike his father, Luis, he hadn't had a vocation. His business had grown organically. But he liked picking up other people's businesses and refining them. Acquisitions had clear goals and they were profitable.

Only that wasn't why he wanted Fairlight Holdings.

The reason for that was simple.

Fenella Ogilvy, his birth mother—the woman

who had rejected him at birth—was 'old' Angus Balfour's daughter. She wasn't actively involved in the business—she had a career as a successful TV presenter—but she had shares, as did her two children, and currently her son, the son upon whom she had bestowed her father's name was acting as interim CEO following his grandfather's death sixteen months ago. In short, Fairlight was an old family firm, much like Cavendish and Cox. He had worked on enough acquisitions to know how sentimental people could be about such businesses. And how much it hurt for them to lose control of them...

But Fenella Ogilvy was no businesswoman, and her son was out of his depth. She wanted out, and that made her vulnerable. And he fully intended to take advantage of that vulnerability. He was going to do to her what she had done to him. He was going to take her need and her weakness and turn it against her. Make her trade her family's business, her family's past and future, for cash.

And then he would shut it down. Erase it for ever as she had tried to erase him.

Glancing over at Dove's carefully composed face, he gritted his teeth. But he wasn't about to share the real reason with anyone.

He shrugged. 'I'm interested in anything that can make me money, Alistair.'

Beside him, Dove flinched. Or perhaps it was a trick of the light, he thought a moment later, glancing over at her pale, composed face. Before he could make up his mind, there was a knock on the door, and he watched as Cox's PA stepped into the room, smiling apologetically.

'I'm terribly sorry to interrupt, Mr Silva—' she looked over at her boss '—I have a call for Mr Cox.'

'Can't it wait, Annabel?' Alistair Cox frowned. 'We were just about to start—'

Gabriel held up his hands. 'Please don't refuse on my account,' he said smoothly. 'Ms Cavendish can keep me company—if that's all right with her, of course?'

There was a small, pulsing silence, like a held breath. 'Of course,' she said finally.

Her face was impassive but, watching her small, swift nod, he felt a rush of satisfaction.

'That's sorted, then. No, really,' he added as Alistair started to protest again. 'It's not often that I get the opportunity to mix business with pleasure, so you'll be doing me a favour, Alistair.' He glanced over to the bottles of still and sparkling water on the table. 'Perhaps we might have some coffee—'

As the door closed the room fell silent, and just like that they were alone.

His heart was suddenly hammering inside his chest. *So this was it.* He had imagined this moment so many times inside his head. Had thought of all the clever, caustic things he'd say. Only now his mind was blank.

Stalling, he moved past her, taking his time, walking with slow, deliberate steps, sensing her gaze on him. And that—her need to track his progress—calmed him, for it meant that she was feeling this too.

He stopped in front of some portraits, tilting his head to read the small brass plaques beneath them, then turned slowly to where Dove stood motionless, her grey eyes fixed on a point past his shoulder. Not that it mattered, he thought, anger pulsing over his skin. Sooner or later she was going to realise that he wasn't going to disappear this time.

Not until he'd got what he came for.

'Beautiful view.' He nodded to the tree-lined cruciform-shaped gardens outside the windows. 'And not just beautiful... Apparently green encourages elevated levels of alertness and vitality.'

Her eyes locked with his. Grey, on the other hand, he thought, was a cloaking colour, designed to hide and obscure. He felt his heart tighten around the shard of ice that had been lodged there ever since Dove had cast him into the wilderness. If only he'd known that six years ago.

She was staring at him in silence, and he waited just as he had waited in that hotel bar. Only this time she was the one who didn't know what was happening. Didn't know that she was about to be chewed up and spat out. But she would...soon enough.

'What are you doing here, Gabriel?' Her voice was husky, but it was hearing her say his name that made his breathing jerk.

'I've told you what I'm doing,' he said softly. Up close, he could see the dilation of her pupils and the flecks of gold in her irises and, unable to resist the cool fury in her eyes, he took a step closer. 'I'm buying Fairlight Holdings.'

Their eyes met. 'And what? You just randomly picked Cavendish and Cox to act on your behalf?'

No, he thought. There had been nothing random about it. It had been a deliberate choice. It had to be that particular law firm.

He stared down at her as the silence between them lengthened. Her cheeks were flushed and the morning sun looked like glitter in her hair. His breath stalled, his groin hardening as he remembered how it had felt to tangle his fingers through its silken weight, to wrap it around her throat and draw back her head to meet his mouth—

Redirecting his thoughts to the matter in hand, he shrugged. 'I was told that Cavendish and Cox were meticulous, diligent and reliable.' He glanced pointedly around the empty war room and frowned. 'But I'm starting to wonder if I was upsold—'

Her chin jutted forward, just as if she was wanting to be kissed, but her eyes were the colour of storm clouds and he could practically see lightning forking across the irises.

'Alistair is the best corporate lawyer in London.'

He had never heard her speak with such vehemence before, and he didn't like the tightness in his chest that it provoked. Maybe that was why he couldn't quite keep the taunting inflection from his voice when he said, 'I could almost believe you mean that—which is surprising, given that loyalty isn't one of your strong points. What, I wonder, did the estimable Alistair Cox do to earn such devotion?'

'He doesn't lie.' She took a step backwards. 'I want you to leave.'

The pulse at the base of her throat was leaping against the pale skin and he felt something pinch inside him, but he shook his head slowly. 'That's not going to happen.'

'Then I'll leave.' Her voice was faint, but firm, in the vast, sunlit room, and he could hear the anger rippling underneath the clipped consonants.

Hear it and feel it in all the wrong places.

His teeth on edge, his eyes held hers. She wasn't going anywhere. And yet part of him—a very specific part—almost wanted her to walk away, so he could see her move again on those teetering red-soled heels that added another four inches to her memorably endless legs. Watch her hips sway in the fitted blue pencil skirt that skimmed her delicate curves.

As she made to move past him he stepped in front of her. 'That's not going to happen either.'

She glared at him, her glossy blonde ponytail quivering like a cat's tail. 'You know, this whole big-shot, ruthless tycoon schtick is starting to wear a little thin. I don't take orders from you.'

You will, he thought, feeling his body respond to the challenge in her words and the small upward tilt of her chin.

Holding her gaze, he shrugged. 'Your surname

might be above the door, Ms Cavendish, but you're just a cog in a wheel.'

There was a second of absolute silence.

'And you're an imposter.'

She sounded as if she had been running. Or been winded.

'And one of these days the whole world is going to realise that. Because you might have money now, Mr Silva, but you don't have class.'

The disdain in her voice snatched at his already fraying temper, but he was grateful. This was the real Dove Cavendish. And he needed to see the snobbish, careless woman who hid behind that beautiful, serene mask.

'And *you* don't have a choice.'

He felt suddenly calmer than he had in weeks. This was it. The moment he had been waiting for. He wanted to see the dawning recognition in those grey eyes that the trap had been sprung and there was no escape.

'You see, six years ago I made a mistake. I thought our relationship had run its course. But I was wrong. I've realised now that you and I have unfinished business. Can you see where this is going, Dove?' He kept his eyes on her face, wanting, needing to enjoy every quiver of shock, every shudder of understanding. 'I think you can. You always were smart.'

Now she was shaking her head. 'I am *not* working for you.'

'You already are.' Watching two streaks of colour

wing along her cheeks, he felt a sharp sting of satisfaction. 'As of this moment, you are in charge of managing the Fairlight acquisition.'

CHAPTER TWO

HE DELIVERED THIS statement almost casually, but his words hit her like a wrecking ball. In charge of the Fairlight acquisition?

Dove stared at Gabriel in stunned silence.

She couldn't feel her face, but her body was so tense she felt as if she might suddenly snap and fly apart into a million pieces. What was he talking about? Had he completely lost his mind? How could he think that she would work for him after what he'd done to her? After the hurt he'd inflicted?

On her way to the war room she had told herself that seeing him again was just something to be endured, and then ended as soon as was legitimately possible. That for some reason—most likely curiosity—Gabriel Silva wanted to see the woman he had conned and cast aside. And after the shock and panic had worn off a part of her had almost welcomed the encounter. She wanted to show him she hadn't crumbled, that she was managing just fine without him.

But it had only been meant to last a moment. She

wasn't supposed to become part of his work with Cavendish and Cox.

She pressed her nails into her palms. Surely he wasn't being serious.

'This is some kind of joke, right?' Heart hammering, she searched his face, but Gabriel wasn't laughing or smiling. He was simply staring at her steadily, calmly, like a chess player who knew that the endgame had been reached.

Finally he shook his head slowly, his piercing blue gaze never leaving her face. 'I never joke about business.'

And now her heart felt as if it was going to burst through her ribs. A fresh shudder of panic raced through her. 'But you can't seriously expect me to work for you,' she said slowly.

'Why not?' He tilted his head up and a shaft of sunlight carved a shadow across his profile.

Why not? His words spun slowly inside her head like a car skidding on black ice. How could he even ask that question? Had he forgotten everything that had happened between them? The lies. The betrayal. The pain.

Her pain—not his.

She felt her stomach lurch. For him, it had only ever been for show. And yet even now, six years after she'd discovered the truth, it was still so hard for her to believe that all of it—the way his eyes had softened when he'd looked at her, the catch in his breath as he'd kissed her throat—had been a lie. It had felt so real at the time. And it had been real for her—achingly, agonisingly real.

But she had too much pride to raise that with him. And what would be the point? He didn't love her. He never had. So there was absolutely no way she was going to hint at how she had loved him.

There was a knock at the door and Becky, one of the office juniors, stepped into the room. She was holding a tray, and Dove saw the delicate Wedgwood china cups and saucers that were Alistair's favourite, and almost certainly irreplaceable. But she suspected that wasn't why Becky's hands were shaking.

'Thank you, Becky.'

'Mr Cox said to let you know that he'll be along shortly.' Becky's cheeks were flushed, and she sounded slightly breathless—as if she was about to faint. Which meant that she had also Googled Gabriel Silva earlier, and was now stunned to discover that his face matched the impossible flawless perfection of his online image.

Dove gritted her teeth as Becky put down the tray.

Be careful what you wish for, she wanted to shout at the younger woman. *Looks aren't everything*.

With those blue eyes and high, hard cheekbones, he might resemble an angel, but he was cruel and dangerous and utterly without conscience. And, yes, she knew that was probably true of a lot of their clients, but this was personal.

To her, anyway.

As the door closed, she turned to face him. 'Don't

do that,' she snapped. 'Don't pretend you don't un-derstand what I'm talking about.' Six years ago she might have been like a puppet on a string, blithely dancing to her doom, but that young woman didn't exist any more. 'You know exactly why I can't work for you.'

She stumbled over the words. But then she shouldn't even be having this conversation. After a normal break-up most people wanted to avoid their exes at all costs. But theirs had not been a normal break-up. Or a normal relationship, she thought, her heart twisting with misery.

Her pulse quivering in her throat, she watched as he pulled out one of the chairs and sat down, stretch-ing out his legs just as if he owned the building and this was *his* war room. Except wars required armies, and this was just the two of them, locked in combat like gladiators trading blows.

She tensed as his eyes flicked up to her accus-ing face.

'I take it you're referring to our history?' he said softly.

History. Her breathing jerked and, lifting a hand protectively to her throat, she felt her pulse pound against her fingers. It was such a soft, vague term for something that had been so deliberately brutal.

She gave a humourless laugh. 'You're damn right I am.'

'What happened—happened.' In the sunlight, his handsome face was suddenly as harsh and unyielding as a statue. 'It's in the past, and I'm willing to leave it there.'

For a moment Dove couldn't breathe. *He* was willing to leave what happened between them in the past?

It was almost impossible to stop herself from grabbing him by the perfectly tailored lapels of his suit, hauling him to his feet and shaking him hard. Did he not know how much she had loved him? Or care about the pain he had caused? Her wide grey eyes fixed on his face as his careless indifference clawed at her throat.

Of course not. And that was why it was so simple for him to forget what hadn't happened.

It wasn't for her.

Stomach in freefall, she silently replayed the years that had passed. Years spent trying to come to terms with the reality of their brief one-sided relationship. Working every night until her head ached and her vision blurred, and then working out at the gym, pounding the treadmill until she was too exhausted to think or remember or, most important of all, feel. Because that was the only way she could carry on.

By not feeling.

None of which would be relevant to Gabriel because he didn't have feelings. Nor did he care about other people's feelings either. As she knew only too well, all he cared about was money.

Outside, the sun was rising higher in the sky, and for a moment she watched its slow ascent, grateful for the reminder that not everything was subject to the will of Gabriel Silva. Then, lifting her chin, she returned his gaze full-on.

'Well, I can't,' she said stiffly. 'So I'm afraid you'll have to ask someone else to manage your acquisition.'

There was a long, heavy silence. Around her the huge meeting room seemed to shrink and grow airless, so that it was suddenly difficult to breathe.

'I didn't *ask* you to work for me,' he replied, and her stomach curled at the clipped ferocity in his voice. 'I told you it was going to happen.'

She shook her head—more to clear it than out of defiance—and he lifted his chin, looking past her in that way of his that already felt too familiar, as if her opinions and wishes were irrelevant to him. Which, she realised with a thump of panic, they clearly were.

'You know, this is all going to be so much harder if you fight me every step of the way. And there's really no point.'

She felt the hairs stand up on the nape of her neck as his brilliant blue eyes fixed on her face.

'You *will* end up working for me.'

She stared over to where he sat—no, lounged in his chair, like some bored potentate who was regretting his decision to grant an audience to one of his minions. He had unbuttoned his jacket and she could see the outline of contoured muscle pressing against his shirt. It was a tantalising hint of what lay beneath.

Not that she needed reminding. She knew exactly what he looked like beneath that crisp, tailored cotton.

A beat of heat danced across her skin. A heat and an awareness, a hunger, she hadn't felt in a long, long time. As if her body was waking from a deep sleep. Only how could that be true? How could she feel anything for this man other than loathing?

'Why are you doing this?' she asked hoarsely, batting those questions to the dark outer reaches of her mind.

His startlingly blue eyes lifted to hers, and the coolness there was such a contrast to her own fraught feelings that she had to clench her hands tightly to stop herself reaching down and hurling the fine bone china cups at his head.

'For the same reason I do everything,' he said, getting to his feet with the leopard-like grace that characterised every moment he made.

'Because I can.'

She couldn't breathe for a moment. Was that what had happened six years ago? Had he taken her father's money simply because it had been offered? Or had he been angling for that all along? It was on the tip of her tongue to ask him. But she didn't want to talk about the past with this cold-eyed stranger.

She licked her lips. 'That's not an answer.'

His eyes homed in on her mouth like a heat-seeking missile tracking its target and she felt the tension throb between them. But then, just as swiftly, he turned away without replying.

Watching him walk across a room six years ago, she had fallen in love with him. Now, though, she stared in appalled fascination as he sauntered slowly round the table. Her eyes fixed to the dark jacket that stretched endlessly across his back and she felt a tic of heat pulse across her skin. Once upon a time she had loved to slide her fingers over the smooth muscles of his shoulders, guiding his movements, her breath staccato in her throat as he drove into her—

Heat bloomed inside her as a blurry montage of their entwined bodies wove through her head...

'So this is him? The guy you're related to?'

Blinking, she glanced over to where Gabriel was standing in front of the gilt-framed portrait of Arthur Cavendish.

She nodded. 'He's my great-great-great-grandfather.'

'Handy. To have a ready-made corporate law firm in the family.' He turned and stared at her, long and hard, a muscle working in his stubble-covered jaw. 'Although I seem to remember you telling me on more than one occasion that you would never work at Cavendish and Cox.' His mouth slanted into a smile that was more of a baring of teeth. 'But perhaps you didn't mean what you said.'

Resentment surged through her, and anger—a hot, sweeping anger such as she had never felt in her life before, so that she wasn't even sure it *was* anger. 'We both said things we didn't mean, Gabriel.' Her eyes met his, grey clashing with the blue. 'And you weren't the only one who made a mistake.'

He didn't like that. She saw the flare of male pride and arrogance in his eyes. But she didn't care. Even if it was too little, too late, she wanted him to hurt—wanted to hurt him as he had hurt her…was still hurting her.

'So now we both know where we stand, why don't you stop with the games—?'

'You think this is a *game*?'

His dark brows snapped together and she took an immediate, defensive step back, her hand rising instinctively in front of her body as he made his way back around the table.

'You think this is a game?' he repeated as he stopped in front of her.

She forced herself to hold her ground.

'I don't know what this is, but I do know that if it was up to me I'd tell you exactly what you could do with your acquisition.'

'Then it's fortunate for all your colleagues that it's Alistair who's in charge of Cavendish and Cox and not you.' His blue gaze held steady and the tension in her stomach wound tighter. 'In case it's passed you by, he's running a business—not a charity. So I doubt he'll be turning away wealthy clients any time soon.'

'But that's where you're wrong.'

She took a step closer, pushing her hand against the solid wall of his chest to emphasise her point. It was harder than she remembered, and warm through his shirt.

'Alistair's not just a lawyer. He's a man of principle. He cares about the way things get done, the way people behave, because he knows that there's more to business than making money. Not that I'd expect a man like you to understand that.'

'And what kind of man is that, Ms Cavendish?'

He leaned into her hand and the touch of him, at once familiar and forbidden, scorched her fingers. She jerked them away.

'A ruthless, amoral, cold-blooded one.'

She flung the words at him, wishing they were sticks or stones, or better still rocks, but instead of hitting their target they seemed to lose their force, like waves hitting a breakwater. And, gazing up, she saw something in his eyes that made her spine tense.

'You forgot successful. But you're working here, so I can understand why *that* word might have been dropped from your vocabulary.'

How dare he say that? Angry words bubbled up in her throat. Maybe the firm was no longer the legal powerhouse it had once been, but it was still a solid, reputable business.

'Cavendish and Cox have been in existence for nearly two hundred years,' she snapped. 'I'd call that pretty successful.'

Watching his mouth twist, she felt her stomach clench. So many smiles, each one different and infinitely more disturbing than the last. This one was doing something strange to the air, making it quiver as if a storm was approaching.

Or maybe the storm was already here, she thought

as he stared down at her, his blue gaze glittering in the sunlight, bright and sharp like tempered steel.

'And yet word on the street is that Cavendish and Cox is going under.'

For a few half-seconds she had that same sensation as earlier, as if she was floating outside her own body. Whatever she had been expecting him to say, it hadn't been that.

Her heart thumped hard inside her chest as she remembered the conversation she'd overheard in a bar. It had been several months ago now. A couple of lawyers from a rival firm had been discussing office space, and one of them had said he had heard that the Cavendish and Cox building was going on the market.

In a panic, she had confronted Alistair, but he'd been unperturbed, almost amused.

'It's just gossip. Honestly, I've lost count of the number of times that this place has supposedly been up for sale.' He had patted her arm reassuringly. 'Things get a little sticky sometimes, but we always get through it, Dove.'

And she had believed him. Selfishly, she'd wanted to believe him—because she couldn't face thinking about what it would mean if he was wrong. She couldn't deal with yet another loss.

But what if he *was* wrong?

A shiver of panic scuttled down her spine.

What if Alistair had lied to her?

Fighting for calm, fighting for control, trying desperately to hold on to her anger and keep the panic at bay, she met Gabriel's gaze. 'I don't know what stone you were under when you heard that particular rumour, but you're mistaken,' she said crisply, as if she wasn't the least bit shaken. 'Everything is fine.'

His face was impassive, but the sudden glint in his eyes sent a dizzying drumroll of adrenaline pounding through her veins.

'Maybe it is,' he agreed, but there was a taunting softness to his voice that made her shiver inside.

'That's the trouble with rumours. Once they're out there…' his gaze shifted momentarily to the tree-lined square outside the window '…they get a life of their own. All it would take would be one high-profile, wealthy client to walk away or perhaps express his concerns—privately, of course—to some of his other equally high-profile and wealthy friends and all of this—' his eyes snapped back to her face '—would come tumbling down like a house of cards.'

The air thumped out of her lungs and she felt her face drain of colour. The room was suddenly silent. Outside in the street even the traffic stilled, as if he had cast a spell over the whole of Lincoln's Inn Fields.

'You wouldn't—'

He must be bluffing.

But she knew from the tiny pause before he answered that he wasn't.

In fact, she was certain he would have no compunction in making good on his threat, and it was all too easy in that moment to remember why, and how much, she hated him.

He looked at her assessingly. 'I wouldn't want to. And I won't have to. Just so long as we're on the same page.'

'And what page is that?'

'Now who's playing games?' he said softly. But his face was hard like polished bronze.

Stiffening her shoulders, she forced her gaze up to his. 'I'm not. I just don't understand why you would want me to work for you.'

'Isn't that obvious?'

The question was accompanied by a careless, deliberately provocative lift of his broad shoulders. 'This acquisition is particularly important to me, so it's vital that I have someone managing it who is as invested as I am. I need someone whose commitment to making it happen matches mine. You're that person.'

She gave a trembling ghost of a laugh. 'You think *I'm* that person?'

Her heart was racing, and the dampness of her hands had nothing to do with the warm morning sunshine filling the room. This was insane. *He* was insane—he must be if he thought that was possible.

Her chin jerked upwards. 'The only thing I'm invested in, Gabriel, is never having to see you again.'

He looked at her, his gaze impassive. 'So you don't mind if Alistair loses the business? The business founded by your great-great-great-grandfather.

You don't care about his legacy? Or about all the people who will lose their jobs?'

The challenge in his voice danced lightly over her skin, making her insides prickle with anger—and something softer and more treacherous.

'Of course I do.'

He shrugged almost lazily. 'Then I've no doubt you will do the very best job you can for me. Because if you don't I will ruin this business. I will drive it into the ground.'

Tears stung her eyes and she blinked them away. She wanted to scream and keep on screaming. At him, and at a world that allowed a man like him to become powerful. Only his words had sucked all the air from her lungs.

'This is how you do business, is it?' she said finally. 'By issuing threats, bullying people, blackmailing them?'

'I do whatever needs to be done to get what I want,' he said, and it was the softness in his voice that made her understand just how ruthless he was.

She glared at him. 'You know, I wish I could say this was a revelation—a hitherto unforeseen glimpse into your character—but frankly it doesn't surprise me at all—'

She broke off, hating herself for becoming so emotional, for letting him get under her skin. Hating him for coming back and tearing down another set of illusions—that she was getting on with her life. In reality she had simply been ignoring a huge, jagged wound...pretending it was healed.

He took a step closer, and every single nerve-ending in her body jerked into life as she breathed in the masculine scent that had been tormenting her ever since she'd walked into the war room.

'This isn't business, Dove.'

His voice rolled through her, fierce and dark and compelling. Or perhaps it was the sound of her name in his mouth as his gaze held her captive.

'This is personal.'

She stared up at him, panic stampeding through her veins, her muscles clenching, tightening hard around the hollow at the bottom of her stomach. Earlier, she had been wrong. He had changed. Now he didn't have to hide who he was any more. He didn't need to pretend or play games. Now he was a man who openly pursued what he wanted. A man not used to failing.

But he was going to fail this time. Because there was no way she was going to work for him. Not without a fight.

'Like I said earlier, we have history.'

Her train of thought snapped in two as images of that 'history' popped into her head. It had been frenzied. *She* had been frenzied. Frantic. Out of control. And strong and hungry and demanding in a way she wasn't in life. Gabriel had released a side to her she hadn't known existed. His kiss had stirred her, his touch unravelled her, and her body had ached at his absence—

It still did.

Her pulse quivered. Because he had left her. In exchange for money. And that was what she needed to focus on and remember. Not this strange, shimmering weave of tension between them that made her heart pound high up in her throat and her body shake inside.

'We had a relationship. We were going to elope. Then my father offered you money to walk away, and you took the money and walked. So, in fact, we don't just have a *history*, Gabriel. What we have is a conflict of interests.'

He was shaking his head, certainty etched into the contoured arcs and planes of his gorgeous face. 'There's no conflict. You want Cavendish and Cox to be around for another two hundred years, and I want that too. All you have to do to make that happen is manage one small acquisition for me.'

And look into his beautiful lying eyes every day and relive the pain and misery of his deceit.

She didn't have a choice. But she tried again.

'Any acquisition is a complex process.' She kept her voice calm and professional. 'As you know, there are multiple steps. At Cavendish and Cox, we believe that communication at each stage of the process is the most important factor in achieving the optimum outcome for our clients.'

His fine dark brows arched. 'So it says on the website. What's your point?'

'How do you expect us to do that?' The slow burn of his gaze made her feel light-headed. Knots were forming in her belly. 'You and I...we don't communicate. On any level. We never did.'

There was a long pause, and the knots inside her tightened as he stood studying her. His blue eyes were so intent it was like being held in a tractor beam. He was so close she could see the ring of darker blue around his irises and the minute constriction of the pupils. Feel the heat and energy and intent humming beneath his immaculate suit.

'I'd have to disagree,' he said finally, breaking the taut silence.

His bright and intensely blue eyes rested on her face, reaching into her, seeing more than she wanted him to see, seeing far too much.

'You see, as I remember it, you and I...we communicated extremely productively,' he said smoothly, but with that same edgy undercurrent that made her head feel light and her nerve-endings judder like telephone wires in a high wind. 'On one level,' he added.

She felt heat spill over her skin, and suddenly her breath was hot and tangled in her throat and she tensed, remembering. Glancing up at his face, she knew from the tension in his jaw that he was remembering it too.

'That was a long time ago.' Her voice sounded scratchy.

Even though it might look like a retreat, she knew that someone as smart as she was supposed to be would have moved out of reach of that tractor beam gaze by now. But it was impossible to stop her own eyes from lingering on his beautiful face and his lush, curving mouth. Impossible not to imagine how that mouth would feel against hers.

He reached out and touched her hair lightly, his thumb brushing against her cheek. 'And yet it feels like only yesterday.'

Heart clattering in her throat, she stared up at him, blindsided by that admission. The sudden roughness in his voice holding her captive just as surely as if he had grasped her wrists, the truth of his words acting like a brake on her anger and panic, so that suddenly her body was incapable of doing anything sensible or sane.

Like pushing his hand away.

Or turning and walking as fast as she could out of the room.

The air quivered, pressing in on them like a force field, and then, before she could chivvy her brain into some kind of response, he bent his head and covered her mouth with his own, just as he'd used to.

Just as if the last six years had never happened.

Just as if she was still his.

The air left her body. Everything stopped, and grew silent. All thought. All awareness. All the barriers she had created. All of it dissolved and there was only the melting heat of his mouth and their banked hunger for one another sweeping through her like the most potent drug.

Around her the room was spinning, blurring the walls into a smear of blue and gold, and instead of sunlight she could see a million stars. Her breath caught as his fingers slid around her waist to the indentation at the small of her back, his thumbs skimming her ribcage, burning her skin through the silk of her blouse. And then she was reaching for the hard, smooth muscles of his shoulders, pulling him closer, flickers of heat skating down her limbs as his lips found the hollow at the base of her throat.

She wanted him so badly she could hardly bear it. Wanted to pull off his clothes, then hers, and press her naked body against his. He must be feeling the same way. Her belly clenched as the tips of his fingers slid over the bare skin of her collarbone and—

A ripple of conversation swelled in the corridor outside and they broke apart as if stung. She stumbled backwards on her heels, gripping the edge of the table, heat pooling in her pelvis, heart running wild.

Gabriel was staring down at her, breathing unsteadily, his eyes blazing. It was some consolation to see that he looked as floored as she felt—but not much.

'We shouldn't have done that,' she said hoarsely. She could hardly string the words into a sentence. Her brain felt dislocated, and she was struggling to pull herself together and catch up with what had just happened. 'Anyone could have walked in.'

There was a tiny shift in the air and something crossed his face—a dark flicker of emotion she couldn't place. And then he was back in control, straightening his cuffs, fixing his gaze on hers, narrowed and so intensely blue it felt like a high tide rushing over her.

'We were lucky.' His mouth curved into a vicious flick. 'But don't worry—I'm not planning on telling anyone. You won't have to pay me to disappear again. Not that you could afford to.'

She stared at him dazedly. Coming so close on the heels of that brief, feverish moment of intimacy, the cool hostility in his voice was as shocking as if he'd slammed a door in her face.

'We can't do this. I can't work for you—'

'Too bad,' he said flatly. 'Life demands sacrifices, Dove. And not even you would be so selfish as to bring down the family business just to spare your ego.'

Her heartbeat was fluttering high in her throat.

But she hadn't been selfish. She hadn't done anything...

'I am so sorry.'

Her head snapped round. Alistair was striding back into the war room, his face flushed with apology. 'I thought I'd be gone five minutes at most.'

She watched Gabriel swing round to face him. 'It's perfectly all right, Alistair. Ms Cavendish has kept me thoroughly entertained. And what's more she has agreed to manage the Fairlight acquisition for me. That is, of course, assuming you can spare her?'

'I can, indeed.' Alistair beamed at her proudly. 'Dove is a very talented lawyer. I can guarantee that you will be impressed by the quality of her work and her dedication.'

'I don't doubt it.'

She felt something complicated happening to her breathing as Gabriel's eyes locked on hers, cool, taunting, daring her to speak, to call his bluff.

'I'll get my people to sort out the paperwork, and we can start prepping on Monday.'

'Wonderful.'

Alistair rubbed his hands together and, sensing his relief, Dove felt a rush of guilt. It wouldn't be obvious to just anyone, but she could see the legacy of fine worry lines fanning out from his mild grey eyes.

Now, though, he was as excited and eager as a child on its birthday. 'I hear the views from your offices are magnificent,' he said to Gabriel.

Dove managed to make a smile appear on her face as Alistair turned to share his excitement. She knew the Silva Group had recently moved into London's latest exclusive high-rise development. A multi-tiered white tower known colloquially as the 'Wedding Cake'. She felt a trickle of relief wash through her, picturing the gleaming open-plan offices. At least there, surrounded by his attentive staff, there would be little opportunity for them to be alone.

'You must come and visit, Alistair. But…' Gabriel paused, and she looked up at him uneasily. 'We won't be working out of the office. You see, when I greenlight an acquisition I prefer to work from *The Argentum*. My yacht,' he added, his eyes on hers. 'She's moored off the Côte d'Azur.'

Her throat was suddenly so tight that it ached to breathe.

Beside her, Alistair was looking even more delighted. 'And you call that working?'

Gabriel inclined his head. 'I know it sounds a little crazy, but it actually works very well. Aside from privacy issues, on shore there are distractions, temptations. Out at sea, everyone stays focused. It's perfect, really.'

The sunlight was behind him now and she couldn't see his expression, just the faint gleam of his eyes. But, staring up at him, Dove felt a warm, slippery panic rising up from her stomach.

Sailing around the Mediterranean while working would be most people's idea of a dream job. Only how was she supposed to stay focused, stay *sane*, when it was clear, after what had happened this morning, that the most distracting temptation for her would not be on shore but on the yacht?

CHAPTER THREE

GABRIEL STRODE OUT into Lincoln's Inn Fields, his blue eyes narrowing. Not at the unusually bright London sunshine but at his complete and utter lack of self-control.

What had he been thinking? Dove Cavendish was the woman who had scorned and then humiliated him. She had taken his heart and trampled on it in her red-soled heels, and yet all it took was one touch and he had forgotten his anger, his thirst for revenge. Had anyone asked him he would have struggled to tell them his name...

His jaw clenched tight, and for a few quivering seconds he could almost feel her body pressed against his as intensely as if it was reality.

Frustration in every sense of the word burned through him.

He had broken his first rule of business. He had let himself get distracted.

But it wasn't as if he had bumped into her randomly in the foyer of some hotel. This day had been long coming. It had taken six long years for everything to fall into place so that he could finally confront Dove Cavendish on her home turf. He had planned it all out, scripted each word, fully intending to cut her down to size, to make her feel as small and powerless as she'd made him feel all those years ago.

Instead, he had behaved like some stupid, oversexed teenage boy.

Holding her in his arms, feeling the fever-heat of her skin beneath that silky blouse, had made time lose its shape so that the past had overlapped the present. In those few devastating seconds when Dove had melted against him it had been as if ten thousand years of evolution had reversed in the blink of an eye. He had no longer been Gabriel Silva, billionaire CEO, whose suits cost the same amount as a small family car. He had been just a man. A primitive man driven by mind-melting impulses and unconscious need.

And that wasn't all. Shaken by his sudden loss of control, and the sweet, wild lightness of Dove's response, he had suggested that she fly out to join him on *The Argentum*—even though, up until that moment, he had been intending simply to keep her dangling in London.

He swore under his breath, then lifted his hand with the mix of carelessness and authority that was now as instinctive to him as breathing, watching as a sleek, dark limousine with tinted windows pulled up alongside the kerb.

Inside the car, the air was cool. Jaw clenching, he sank back against the pale leather upholstery.

It hadn't always been the case. Making money was the easy part—but being rich took surprisingly long to master. Because being rich was about more than just having a lot of money. And he had a *lot* of money. More than he could have ever imagined, growing up in his parents' two-bedroomed terraced house in Swindon.

Some of the tension in his shoulders loosened, as it always did when he thought about his mother and father. Luis and Laura Silva might not have had much money, but they had given him everything a son could want or need. They had supported and guided him and had faith in him. Most of all they'd loved him—unconditionally.

Once upon a time, when he had been younger and more trusting, he had believed Dove loved him like that too. He knew better now.

He pressed the heel of his hand against his forehead, then closed his eyes, seeing again the look of panic on her face as they broke apart. For her, it had never been a relationship. It had been just a summer fling. Maybe she'd liked it that he'd been nothing like any of the men in her circle, with their floppy fringes, striped shirts and loud, braying voices. That summer, when he'd worked as a waiter for an events company, he'd had his fill of them. He had thought Dove had too. It was certainly what she'd implied.

But what had he really known about her?

His eyes snapped open.

Nothing, that was what.

More incredibly still, he hadn't cared. The first time he'd laid eyes on Dove, he'd wanted her. Wanted her more than he had ever wanted anything or anyone. Wanted her so badly that it had hurt to breathe.

He had been working since the start of the summer. Sometimes in the kitchens, scraping food from pots and pans, loading plates and cutlery into the dishwashers. Other times he'd been required 'front-of-house' to wait at tables. All of it had been dull, repetitive, exhausting work, but he'd needed money—he'd always needed money then. And he had still been smarting from what had happened a year earlier. Work had taken his mind off the pain. And the guilt.

And the shame.

The shame of failing. Failing to be wanted, welcomed, embraced. Not once but twice.

Truthfully, he'd been a mess—only then Dove had walked into his marquee. Dazzling, flawless, untouchable. With her gleaming pearl-blonde hair streaming down her back and those soft kissable lips parted in an extraordinarily sweet smile that had spread like nitrous oxide through his limbs.

And she had been so much more than the sum of her parts. She'd been smart—book-smart—but also curious about the world beyond hers. And her voice… She'd had a beautiful voice…soft and precise and hypnotic.

Just like the touch of her fingers, he thought, his pulse quickening.

His own fingers bit into the leather upholstery. He had been so certain she was the one. And, fresh from Fenella Ogilvy's brutal rejection, he had been hungry to be seen, recognised. To be wanted, heard, needed…

Instead, for the second time in his life, he had been paid to disappear. He'd become yet another dirty little secret to be buried. And he had felt not just rejected but buried alive.

His gaze drifted to the window, to where a woman with a blonde ponytail was jogging along the pavement. His pulse accelerated, as if to keep pace with her stride. He hadn't felt as if he was buried alive back in that war room. On the contrary, his need for her had been like a roar of flame and lava beneath his skin.

Remembering Dove's face, the restless heat in her eyes and the flushed cheeks, he felt his groin tighten. He swore softly, yanked his tie loose from his neck and tossed it across the back seat, wishing he could tear off the rest of his clothes.

Or go back and tear off hers.

His whole body tensed, and before he could stop himself, he was picturing a naked Dove, splayed out on the oversized table in the war room, blonde hair spilling over her pale shoulders, mouth parted—

Groaning, he smacked his head back against the padded upholstery—and then he caught sight of his driver's eyes in the rear-view mirror and checked himself.

That wasn't going to happen.

It was true he had lost control earlier, but that was understandable. Seeing her again had been a shock, and that shock had momentarily swept aside everything. Erasing their history as if it had never happened. Changing his priorities so that in those few febrile seconds he had effectively been a blank slate.

Put like that, was it any surprise that some kind of muscle memory had kicked in?

He tapped on the glass behind his driver's head. 'Take me back to the hotel.'

Kissing her had been inevitable—necessary. Cathartic, in a way. But it would be different next time.

Feeling calmer, he sank back in his seat. Everything was still on track. And now he was just one very long, very cold shower away from purging Dove Cavendish from his body for ever.

As the sleek white helicopter rose up into the sky, hovering momentarily like a seagull riding a thermal air current, Dove felt her stomach flip. This was it. After nearly a week of pretending this might never happen, she was now just minutes away from seeing Gabriel again.

Living with him.

Working for him.

It was five days since he had waltzed back into her life and effectively shaken it like a snow globe. Now, to all appearances, everything was settled and calm again. The letter of engagement had been signed and Alistair was humming to himself as he walked the corridors.

She leaned her head back against the seat.

But beneath her pale skin chaos reigned.

Twisting slightly, she gazed down. Beneath her, the legendary Château Saint-Honoré was shrinking, turning into a dolls'-house-sized palace beside the glittering Mediterranean. A syncopated beat of panic and anger drummed across her skin as she watched the coastline disappear. If it had been anyone else footing the bill she would have enjoyed staying at the Saint-Honoré. The hotel was eye-poppingly opulent, sun-soaked, *soignée*—a one-of-a-kind testament to Riviera grandeur, harking back to a time when European aristocrats and Hollywood film stars had wintered by the famous pool with its dramatic black and white tiles.

But she suspected that the lavishness of her accommodation had simply been Gabriel's way of reminding her yet again that he was calling the shots.

Her hand tightened around the leather armrest.

First, she had been invited to his offices at the 'Wedding Cake', to meet with his team—including his intimidatingly polished and articulate chief operating officer, Carrie Naylor. Then there had been a chauffeur-driven limousine that had appeared like Cinderella's carriage to ferry her to the airport, where a sleek, snub-nosed private jet had sat waiting for her on the Tarmac to take her to the most exclusive hotel in the French Riviera.

And now she was in a helicopter, flying to *The Argentum*.

All thanks to the 'generosity' of Gabriel Silva.

The only consolation was that the man himself had been conspicuously absent. Apparently *'unwinding in Paris'*.

She sucked in a breath. Carrie had let that slip. And it shouldn't have mattered. It shouldn't have hurt. Only it did.

Everything hurt. Seeing him again. Having him back in her life but *not* back in her life. He was a stranger, and yet he knew things about her that no one else knew. So much had happened between them—only everything she'd felt had been false. For Gabriel it had all been just a game. And now she was going to have to work with him.

Her shoulders stiffened against the cool leather. When Dove was a child, her mother had used to read her the Greek myths. Some she'd loved, like the tale of the Golden Apple, but the one she'd hated was the story of Theseus and the Minotaur. Only it hadn't been the monster that had scared her, but the labyrinth. She hadn't been able to bear to imagine how it would feel to be trapped in the darkness, blundering into one dead end after another.

She didn't need to imagine it now.

Ever since Gabriel had left the office she had been trapped in a labyrinth of his making. She had tried repeatedly, and unsuccessfully, to find a loophole—she was a lawyer, after all. But unless she was willing to call his bluff there was no way out.

And she couldn't do that. She couldn't risk doing something that might harm Alistair. Or the fifty or so people who worked at Cavendish and Cox. And then, of course, there was Olivia. Refusing to work for Gabriel would have meant telling Alistair the truth about Gabriel and Oscar, and then her mother would have found out everything—because that was how it worked. One moment of transparency would lead inevitably to another, like flowers bursting into bloom in spring.

After all this time, could she really just casually drop that kind of grenade in her mother's lap? It would serve no purpose except to upset her, and Olivia was finally in a good place.

'Not long now, Ms Cavendish.'

Her chin jerked up. The helicopter's co-pilot had turned to face her, smiling reassuringly.

'We should see *The Argentum* in around ten minutes.' His eyes dropped to where her hand was clamped around the armrest. 'Would you like me to play some music through the speakers? Some of our more nervous passengers have found it helpful not to hear the sound of the rotors.'

She smiled stiffly. 'Thank you.'

Moments later, soft piano music filled the cabin

and, uncurling her fingers, she rested her hands in her lap. She wasn't a nervous flyer. But there was no need to tell a perfect stranger the truth. That the real reason for her nervousness was sitting on *The Argentum*.

All six foot four of him.

Nothing short of a medicated coma was going to make this terrible edgy feeling disappear. Not when she could still feel the imprint of his lips against hers.

She felt a sharp warning twist through her stomach, like seasickness, just as if she was already standing on the deck of the yacht. But in her mind she was back there in the war room, replaying the moment when Gabriel had kissed her.

It shouldn't have happened—she had been right about that. But being right with hindsight didn't change the facts. He had kissed her, and she had let him. Worse, she had kissed him back.

Why had she done that?

There was no making sense of it. But that hadn't stopped her from asking herself that question roughly every ten minutes since Gabriel had sauntered out of the Cavendish and Cox building five days ago. The only difference was that this time it was asked to the accompaniment of Chopin's *Prelude Op 28 No 15*.

And she still didn't have an answer—or at least not one that didn't make her want to jump out of the helicopter and into the sea below.

Glancing out of the window, she felt her heart start to beat arrhythmically. But it was too late even for that now.

Beneath her, a glossy white yacht rose out of the shimmering sheet of water like a displaced iceberg. Stomach churning, she pressed her hands together in her lap to hide how badly they were shaking. Back at the hotel, she'd thought Gabriel had deliberately already taken the yacht out to sea for some Machiavellian reason designed to put her in her place. But now she saw there could be only few marinas that would be able to take a boat of that size.

'She's beautiful, isn't she?'

Turning her gaze, she saw that both pilots were gazing down at *The Argentum* with undisguised admiration.

'And not just beautiful,' the co-pilot added. 'That bow can cut through Arctic ice.'

'That's amazing.' Dove smiled automatically. It was the kind of detail Alistair would have loved, and she felt a sharp pang, picturing his excitement when she told him.

The helicopter began to descend, just as she had known it would, and ten minutes later she was stepping onto the sleek white deck, panic punching through her like a jackhammer. She was half expecting Gabriel to meet her—not out of courtesy, but simply to gloat. Instead, a short, bright-eyed man wearing navy trousers and a white polo shirt greeted her with a firm, dry handshake. In his other hand he was holding a tablet.

'Welcome on board *The Argentum*, Ms Cavendish. I'm Peter Reid, the chief steward. Did you have a good flight?'

'Yes, thank you. It was very...' she searched for an adjective '...smooth.'

'That's what we aim for.' Lifting the tablet, he typed something, then swiped across the screen. 'Just updating the manifest,' he murmured. 'Now, if you would like to come this way, Mr Silva is waiting for you in the lounge.'

She followed him through the boat, the sound of her heartbeat swallowing up his voice intermittently so that she only caught occasional snatches of sentences.

'...sixty-member crew...twenty thousand square feet of living space...encased in bomb-proof glass... fingerprint security system...twenty-four thousand horsepower diesel engines.'

It sounded more like a floating high-security prison than a boat, she thought, panic swelling in her throat.

As they stopped in front of a door, the steward turned and smiled. 'We can outrun almost anything on the high seas—including pirates. Although that's not something we have to worry about in this region.'

He knocked briskly on the door, and without waiting for a reply opened it.

Dove stepped reluctantly into the room. Frankly, the idea of coming face to face with a pirate was not nearly as unsettling as the sight of the man standing on the other side of the room with his back to her, gazing out to sea.

Only this time it was going to be different, she told herself firmly. There would be no sliding back in time, no picking over the bones of the past. She would be cool, calm and professional.

But as Gabriel turned slowly to face her, her heart lurched like a scuttled ship.

Five days ago, when this moment had been simply a concept, she had thought that it would be easier seeing him the second time. She'd been wrong. If anything, she was having to fight a quivering, betraying flush as he walked towards her, shockingly beautiful in dark suit trousers and a pale blue shirt.

'So, you made it, then?'

As he stopped in front of her she forced her eyes up to meet his, and for a moment she thought she saw a flicker of admiration or respect. But then it was gone, and he was gesturing towards one of the large cream Barcelona chairs that were grouped around a delicate scallop-edged eau-de-nil wool rug.

She took a furtive glance around the room. It was cool and modern and minimal, with sculptural lighting, one vast Cy Twombly canvas in muted shades and ocean views on three sides. It was nothing like the war room at Cavendish and Cox but, judging by the edgy, pulsing tension filling the room, it was still a battleground, she thought, tucking her legs to one side as she sat down.

'I wondered whether you might send someone else in your place.'

His voice was cool, taunting, silky-smooth, and

she couldn't tell if the tightness in her chest was anger or foreboding or confusion. Because she *hadn't* sent her father to find him all those years ago. It had been Oscar's idea to challenge Gabriel—to test his intentions. She didn't know to this day how he had found out about their relationship—it hadn't seemed to matter much in the scheme of things. And, really, what did it matter now what Gabriel had mistakenly thought all those years ago? It was a detail. It wasn't something vast and life-changing...like lying to someone about being in love.

She squared her shoulders. 'I'm not like you, Gabriel. Once I've committed to something I don't change my mind.'

'Nice try.' His tone matched hers, but it was layered with a dark edge that made her legs tremble. 'But we both know the only reason you're here is because you're scared of calling my bluff.'

She swallowed, her hand reaching up to touch the pearls at her throat. Was this how it was going to be? Death by a thousand cuts. Every word, every glance, a fresh blow to parry or contain.

I can't go through with this, she thought, misery gnawing at her insides.

But she knew she would; It was what she'd been trained to do—both as a lawyer and as the daughter of Oscar and Olivia Cavendish.

'I'm not scared of you.'

Oddly enough, she wasn't. Not now that she was here and the danger of him making good on his threat had receded. Mostly she was scared of herself. Or rather she was scared of her body's strange, ungovernable response to his.

As if to prove the point, she felt her gaze drift towards him, drawn irresistibly by the triangle of light gold skin that was visible between the open collar of his shirt.

Stop it, she told herself. *It was only one kiss.*

But even as she shoved the memory aside she felt it prickle beneath her skin.

He raised one, smooth, dark eyebrow. 'Let me guess... This is where you tell me all about how you've worked with far more demanding and difficult clients than me.'

'Actually, I don't see you as a client,' she said crisply, her pulse flicking back and forth like a flame in a draught. 'To me, you're just a bully. A rich man without scruples. A man who uses his wealth and power to get what he wants.'

His pupils flared, turning his blue eyes into dark, fathomless pools. For a moment he didn't reply. He just let the silence and the tension build between them, swallowing up the air so that she thought she might never breathe again.

'Not *everything* I want,' he said finally. 'Or have you forgotten what happened in the war room?'

This time the silence was shorter—like a caught breath. Pulse stumbling, she stared back at him, her skin growing hotter and tighter as his gaze meandered slowly over her puffed-sleeve blouse and pencil skirt down to her towering nude court shoes, and her mind replaying the burning heat of his mouth and the hardness of his body against his.

No, she hadn't forgotten—and she suspected that Gabriel knew that. And then his gaze dropped to her mouth, as though he too was reliving those frantic moments when his lips had fused with hers, and she felt heat bloom high in her pelvis, just as if he had reached out and touched her there.

She swallowed…shifted.

It would be so easy to lean in and clasp that beautiful face in her hands, to press her mouth to his and slide her fingers through his silky dark hair and pull him closer, then closer still, until there was no daylight between them. And then his hands would start to move with unimaginable freedom over her body, owning her, claiming her, making her ache inside—

She balled her hands as heat rushed through her and, shaken by this new evidence of her weakness, she dragged her gaze away.

'I haven't forgotten it yet. But from memory it shouldn't take me long,' she said quickly. *Too quickly.*

She could tell from the dark gleam in his blue eyes that he didn't believe her. But then she couldn't blame him for that. She didn't believe herself. Suddenly she felt dizzy, the thought that this was her life now, for however long it took to get the acquisition over the line, making her head spin.

He stared at her for a long, level moment, considering her, weighing up his response. 'Gets under your skin, doesn't it?' he said at last, breaking the taut silence. 'That you still want me.'

A tiny, quivering flicker of heat skated down her spine and she felt her breathing wobble.

She gazed up at him, her throat impossibly dry, feeling the blueness of his eyes like a touch or a caress. He had a wonderful sense of touch…light, but precise. Sometimes before, when they'd been in the car or walking down the street, he would reach over and stroke the nape of her neck, and she would feel it all the way through, just as if she was melting…

Her cheeks were on fire, and she knew that her face must be red, but she would be damned if she was going to agree with him.

'What gets under my skin stopped being your concern a long time ago, Gabriel, so I suggest we put that behind us,' she said crisply. 'After all, you're paying me to work, and I wouldn't want to waste your money. I know it's all that matters to you.'

The air between them seemed to thicken and he stared at her, a muscle pulsing in his jaw, his gaze narrowing on hers in a way that made her breath stop in her throat. Finally, he gave one of those infinitesimally tiny shrugs that made a vortex of emotion rise and swell inside her.

'What else is there?'

Dove blinked. There was no reason that statement should hurt as much as it did, but she couldn't stop a shiver of misery seeping over her skin. And once again, it was as easy to hate him as it was tempting to hurl insults at his handsome head. But, remind-ing herself of her decision not to discuss the past, she changed the subject.

'So, what happens next?'

She felt his gaze sweep over her.

'We start developing strategy tomorrow, after breakfast. My people have already compiled a de-tailed history of Fairlight Holdings—the financials, customer base, et cetera, et cetera… There's a paper copy in your suite. Get acquainted with it.'

She nodded, grateful for the reminder of why she was there. If she could just keep that fact at the front of her mind, and banish all the other stuff, then maybe she would get through this unscathed.

'The rest of the afternoon is yours to do with as you wish.' He paused, his blue gaze resting on her face. 'And tonight it will be just the two of us dining.'

Just the two of us.

Heart pounding fiercely, she stared at him.

Dinner. Alone with Gabriel.

The words whispered inside her and she curled her fingers into the palms of her hands to steady her-self, her mind shying away from an image of the two of them seated beneath a canopy of stars.

'What do you mean, just the two of us?' she said stiffly. 'I thought your team was here.'

It was happening again—that feeling that she was watching things from outside her body, almost as if she was watching a movie with an actor and actress playing herself and Gabriel. She forced air into her lungs.

'Then you thought wrong.' He gave her a razor-edged smile. 'They arrive tomorrow. So, like I said, it will just be the two of us tonight.'

Blood was pounding in her ears. 'I'm really not very hungry.'

It was hard enough being here with him now. But she didn't want to spend any more time with him than was necessary. She certainly didn't want to spend an entire evening with him alone—not after what had happened in London. It would be too close to what they'd once had in the past, when eating together had often been foreplay.

'Marco is a two-star Michelin chef. I'm sure he can conjure up something to tempt you.'

'I'm sure he can—but I don't want to eat dinner with you.' She was shaking her head. Her voice was shaking too, with panic and anger, and she knew she was revealing too much—revealing things she should be trying to keep hidden. But she couldn't seem to help herself.

For a moment Gabriel didn't respond. He just stood there, with the sunshine pouring over his shoulders so that he looked like his celestial namesake. But then the warmth and the light faded and he took a step towards her, and instantly that shimmering thread between them she had been trying hard to ignore pulled tight.

'I don't care.'

His tone more than the words themselves made her flinch. It was so hard and unsympathetic and gut-wrenchingly remote that she felt as if he was talking to her from a script.

'How charming.' She held his gaze as if she wasn't the least bit shaken. 'First threats and now a complete lack of empathy. No wonder you have to blackmail people to work for you.'

He took another step, and now his lean, muscular body was dangerously close to hers.

'I don't know how things are done at Cavendish and Cox, Dove. Maybe your surname means that people go easy on you. But let me be clear about how you and I are going to work—how *this* is going to work.'

His eyes on hers were steady and cool, like deep ocean water...the kind that never felt the warmth of the sun's rays.

'I don't have the time or the patience for theatrics. So if I say you're eating dinner with me, all you need to ask is what time and where? It's eight p.m., by the way, on the owner's deck. The stewards will show you where to go.' He paused, then, 'A word of caution, Dove—of warning, even. I would advise against any pointless displays of temper or defiance. The stakes are too high.'

She watched mutely as he turned and walked back to the window.

'Oh, and shut the door on your way out.'

CHAPTER FOUR

ONCE IN HER SUITE, Dove sank down into a chair. There was a jug of iced water on the table beside her, and she poured a glass and drank it quickly.

She was used to confrontation…to conflict. Her parents' marriage had not just been unhappy, it had been a war zone. Rows had punctuated every day, with the shelling starting over the breakfast table and often continuing long into the night.

They'd both wanted to leave, but Olivia had sunk her inheritance into the Cavendish estate and Oscar had been too lazy to divorce and so they'd stayed married—unhappily, bitterly married. And it had been up to Dove to negotiate the ceasefires between them and act as go-between.

In other words, this wasn't the first time she'd had to grit her teeth and try to stay calm, neutral, unaffected…

Glancing down at her shaking hands, she breathed out unsteadily. Only she didn't feel unaffected. She felt exhausted in the same way that a soldier returning from the trenches must feel. Felt relief, paired with the stifled horror of knowing that at some point in the not too near future she was going to have to go back and face the enemy again.

Only what kind of enemy made you want to lean in closer and touch, caress, kiss...?

She was just trying to think of an answer that wouldn't make her sound mad or foolish or both when her mobile rang. Her bags had been brought to her room and it took her a moment to fish out her phone. She glanced at the screen. It was her mum.

'Hi, Mum—what's up?'

'Nothing, darling. I just wanted to check that you'd got there all right.'

Dove sat down on the bed, toeing off her heels. 'I messaged you yesterday.'

'Yes—to say you were at the hotel. But you said you were flying out to the yacht today and I hadn't heard anything. And I've never liked helicopters. Look at what happened to poor Roddy Conroy.'

'That was a hang-glider, Mum, not a helicopter.'

There was a second of silence and then her mother's laugh filled her ear. 'Oh, yes, that's right—it was.'

Dove laughed too then. It had been a long time since she'd heard Olivia sound upset, but she still got a buzz from hearing the happiness in her mother's voice.

Picturing her father's handsome, petulant face, she felt a pang of guilt. She'd loved both her parents, but her father had often been hard to like. When he could be bothered, Oscar had a great deal of charm, but in private that charm had rarely been visible. Scratch the surface and that beautiful glitter had revealed base metal.

Nobody knew that better than her mother, and the idea of her daughter losing her heart to a man like Oscar was what Olivia dreaded most.

It was why Dove had chosen to keep secret her short, harrowing relationship with Gabriel.

More importantly, it was why she had lied to Gabriel about her parents.

He hadn't talked much about his family, but there had been a softness in his voice when he had, and he had shown her some photos on his phone. She'd been able to tell by their easy body language that his family dynamic was the polar opposite of hers.

She'd felt ashamed and scared. How could she possibly have explained to him her parents' fraught marriage or her own role as referee-cum-counsellor? So she had lied. Just a small white lie at the beginning. But after that she hadn't known how to backtrack to the truth. In the end, it hadn't mattered anyway.

'Everything's fine,' she said soothingly now.

And it wasn't quite a lie, she thought, glancing round her beautiful, understated cabin, with its dazzling, uninterrupted view of the Mediterranean.

'It certainly is.' Her mother's light voice danced with excitement. 'Alistair is just thrilled. So tell me, darling, what's he like, this Gabriel Silva…?'

The question bumped around Dove's head long after her mother had hung up.

Picturing Gabriel's arresting face, she tightened her fingers around the cold glass. Whatever she had expected in London, this was a million times worse. It would be easier if they just hated one another. And sometimes she did hate Gabriel. But at other times she could feel her body reaching out to his, and she knew that he was feeling it too—that knife-edged need that had somehow survived the terrible implosion of their relationship.

It made no sense. But then it wasn't supposed to. Sexual attraction wasn't a science. You couldn't apply logic to it. It supplanted reason, analysis and argument. Her mouth twisted. Apparently, it overrode pain and betrayal too.

Only so what if it did?

Maybe her body's response to him—that alarming, shimmering reaction that swamped her whenever he was near—was impossible to change. But she could change the way she reacted to those feelings. Even if this was personal—and it was—she could make it about business, about the acquisition.

If she wanted to survive this—survive *him*, Gabriel Silva, again—that was what she was going to have to do.

And she would survive, she told herself firmly.

This was a long way from the worst place she had been. A long way from the dark place she'd been in six years ago. So even though his beauty made her catch her breath, she would pretend it didn't. She would pretend as Gabriel had pretended.

After all, how hard could it be?

Gazing across the dazzling indigo sea that was one shade lighter than his eyes, Gabriel felt his pulse slow. He knew the science of 'blue space', but for him there was more to it than just the generic restorative powers of the colour of the water or the sound of the waves. Out here, away from the rigidity of the land, there were no boundaries or barriers. Just an endless vista of blue, stretching unhindered to the horizon and beyond.

Maybe that was why someone like him found it so calming. Having doors shut in your face was not something you forgot.

Or forgave.

He looked away to where a reddish sun was slowly slipping beneath the line of the horizon. After Dove's rejection he'd took a flight to America alone, wanting, *needing* to go somewhere no one would know his past or see his pain.

And it had worked. Living among strangers, he had found his humiliation and misery was invisible to most people. Only his parents and siblings had sensed the change in him. His father, ever the romantic, had put it down to *saudade*—a potent word used by the Portuguese to describe an impossible to translate mix of melancholy and longing. His mother had just thought he was homesick.

But home had not been the solution. In fact, even just thinking about England had made all his symptoms worse. It was work that had helped. Just having a routine, a focus.

But a part of him had never forgotten or forgiven the two women who had rejected him so coolly, so brutally, and six months ago it had been work that had offered up a way for him to avenge himself on both Fenella Ogilvy and Dove Cavendish.

He glanced down at his watch. It was already eight o'clock, but he made no effort to move. He had no qualms about keeping Dove waiting. Why should he? Six years ago she had happily left him sitting in that hotel bar for two hours.

His chest felt suddenly too tight for his ribs. He could still remember the sidelong glances of the bar staff as he'd checked his phone for messages, and then the slow, creeping shift from excitement into apprehension, then panic, and finally shock when Oscar Cavendish had strolled towards him, looking as out of place in the shabby hotel as a Rolls Royce in a scrapyard.

It had been almost a carbon copy of what had happened a year earlier with Fenella Ogilvy, his biological mother. Different hotel bar. Different smiling emissary. But the same conversation. The same mix of politeness and pity. And, of course, a financial incentive for him to disappear for ever.

Only despite all of that—or maybe because of it—he had been as shocked and hurt as the first time it happened. Devastated, in fact. Because Fenella had only ever been a name, whereas he'd thought he knew Dove.

He did now.

He took one last look at the sea and then stepped back into his luxurious suite.

Dove was waiting for him on deck, and even though he knew it was petty, seeing her standing there made him feel immensely satisfied. He glanced over to where she stood, facing the Mediterranean. He couldn't help wishing she had defied him, and he realised that the prospect of sparring with her excited him…made him feel more alive than he had in years.

Why that should be the case was beyond his comprehension. It was certainly not something he had anticipated back in New York, when all of this had been theoretical.

But since then he had summoned her to *The Argentum* and now he was dining with her alone. He hadn't planned that either.

'Good evening, Mr Silva.'

'Good evening, Hélène.'

The stewardess stepped forward, smiling, and as he greeted her, Dove turned towards him.

He felt the air snap to attention. He hadn't told her to do so but she had changed for dinner, into a simple grey sleeveless wrap dress. It was the kind of dress that would make most women fade into the background. But on Dove the silky fabric shimmered like a mountain stream in moonlight.

He stared at her in silence, his gaze skimming over her light curves, his body twitching with a hunger that had nothing to do with the food his chef Marco was preparing at the end of the deck by the teppanyaki grill.

Taken individually, her delicate features were mathematically perfect. But as a whole the effect was breathtaking. Add in the pearl-blonde hair and she was as flawless and untouchable as a goddess. His breath felt suddenly hot and heavy in his throat as his brain reminded him where to kiss her neck, so that her eyes would flutter shut and she would stir restlessly against him, blindly seeking more contact—

'Would you like an aperitif, Mr Silva?'

He turned towards Hélène. 'No, I think we'll sit down. Ms Cavendish, will you join me?'

Dove gave him a smile that could only be described as glacial and nodded. 'Of course.'

Settling into the chair at right angles to her, he watched her reach for a water glass. 'Would you like wine?'

'No, thank you.'

'How is your suite?' he asked softly. 'I hope everything is to your satisfaction?'

Her grey eyes lifted to meet his. 'It is—thank you.'

Her voice was soft and cool, like newly fallen snow, but the way she was sitting told a different story. Every line of her body suggested tension and distance, almost as if she was behind glass, and he knew that she was counting down the seconds until she could leave.

He stared across the table, his teeth suddenly on edge, a tic of irritation pulsing down his spine. Earlier, when she tried to get out of eating with him, he had reacted instinctively, harshly, wanting and needing to demonstrate to her that *he* was in charge this time.

So instead of skulking in her room she was here, sitting at his table, being faultlessly polite.

Only strangely he hated that more.

But why?

His heart thumped against his ribs, but before he had a chance to think too deeply about how to answer that, or why the question even needed to be asked, the stewardess reappeared.

'Today, we have a starter of broad bean, rocket and pecorino cheese salad with a champagne vinaigrette,' she said, carefully sliding plates onto the table. 'Enjoy.'

'Thank you.'

As Dove looked up at the stewardess her face softened, the guarded tension leaving her eyes, and she smiled a smile so genuine, so warm, and of such irresistible sweetness, that for a moment he just stared, transfixed.

And then, remembering the cool, careful smile she had directed at him, he felt as if he had been kicked by a horse. He stared at her in silence, momentarily off-balance, unsure of what to do with the feeling of envy rolling through him. It didn't matter how Dove smiled at him—he knew that. And yet, inexplicably, he wanted her to smile at him like she'd used to.

As if he was everything to her.

Not just a man who used his wealth and power to get what he wanted.

That feeling was another of those things he hadn't anticipated back in New York. But then, back in New York everything had seemed cut and dried, black and white. His eyes locked with hers. *Not grey.*

'So why did you change your mind?' he asked.

Her chin jerked up. 'About what?'

He leaned forward to pick up his glass and caught a whisper of her light floral perfume. 'You wanted to become a barrister. What changed?'

She bit into her lip and then stopped, shrugged. 'I grew up. To be a barrister you need to enjoy arguing your point. You have to get a buzz out of confrontation. And I've had—'

Now she broke off, glancing away to the fragile paper moon that had replaced the setting sun.

'What I'm trying to say is that I worked out that the kind of law I like—the part I enjoy—is the problem-solving, the attention to detail, the academic rigour that goes into crafting an acquisition.'

Crafting. His pulse twitched. Interesting… And certainly not a term you'd find in the average corporate lawyer's word cloud. Should he be surprised, though? Dove had always been a whole lot more than just a pretty face…

Eventually they were drinking coffee, and the stewards had retired to the crew's lounge.

He'd been on other yachts where the crew would be held in limbo at the edges of the deck for hours, stifling yawns while the guests partied on until dawn and then slept in until midday. But he could still remember what it had felt like, waiting endless hours for his shift to end, and it was one of the promises he'd made to himself as his career took off. To treat the people at the bottom with humanity and respect.

Of course, if he needed anything all he had to do was wave his hand across the screen of his phone and one of the stewards would reappear.

He picked up his cup. He'd been pretty sure Dove would refuse coffee, had she been given the choice, but the stewards had brought it out automatically and they had moved to sit on one of the deep modular sofas. Actually, he was sitting. She was standing, feigning interest in the distant lights of another yacht.

Or perhaps she was looking at the stars. They were particularly bright tonight, and Venus was also making an appearance in the night sky.

And on deck too, he thought, his gaze locking on to where Dive was braced against the railing.

Instead of a ponytail her hair was twisted at the nape of her neck with some kind of ornamental stick, and a gentle breeze was catching the loose tendrils that had escaped. In the moonlight, the pearls around her throat gleamed like stars that had fallen to earth. She looked even more like a mythological goddess than before.

She turned to face him. 'I read the report,' she said.

He stared at her blankly. *What report?*

As if that question was written in block capitals across his face, she frowned. 'You suggested I get acquainted with it. So I did.' Her eyes found his reluctantly. 'Whoever compiled it should be congratulated. They did a good job.'

He got to his feet and walked slowly towards her, taking his time. 'That's good to know.' He stopped in front of her, his eyes snagging on the pulse-point hammering beneath the pearl choker. 'I mean, what would be the point of blackmailing them into working for me if I don't get results?' he said softly.

There was a silence. Above them, the dark sky quivered.

A flush of pink was colouring her cheeks. 'I shouldn't have said that.'

He heard the catch in her voice.

'I know it's not true. I've met your staff, and they don't have a bad word to say about you.'

'You sound surprised.'

He studied her profile. From this angle, he could see the knot of hair at the nape of her neck, and suddenly he had to fight against an urge to reach out and pull it loose.

'Can you blame me?' Her eyes met his. 'After all,

we both know the only reason I'm here is because I'm scared of calling your bluff.'

A pulse of heat danced across his skin. Hearing his own words in her mouth felt oddly intimate—distractingly so. There was a hollow, hungry feeling in his stomach, and for a moment it was difficult to get his thoughts in order.

'But you're not scared of me, are you?' he said finally.

Her eyes widened, the pupils flaring like twin stars imploding, and they stared at one another in silence for one long, shattering moment. He could feel his pulse leaping against the light cotton of his shirt and the deck felt unsteady beneath his feet, almost as if it were tilting.

She ducked away from his gaze. Glancing down, he saw that there were goose bumps on her bare arms.

'Are you cold?' Without waiting for a reply, he slid off his jacket and draped it around her shoulders. 'Here.'

I'm fine. I don't need your jacket.' Frowning, she tried to wriggle free of its weight.

His fingers bit into the lapels, pulling it tighter. 'And yet you're trembling.'

'So are you,' she said hoarsely, her hands coming up to grip his arms.

And with shock, he realised he was.

He stared down into her pale upturned face. He could feel the sea breeze through his shirt, but that wasn't why he was shaking. It was her. And he wasn't just shaking. His whole body was throbbing with a desire he had never experienced before.

But even as he was accepting the truth of that thought Dove leaned in and kissed him.

It was nothing like the kiss in London. That had been hard and urgent, with their anger and frustration and the pull of the past combusting with the oxygen in the room to create a sharp flare of light and heat.

This was slower, more tentative. Almost like a first kiss. That stop-start, slow-slow, quick-quick-slow foxtrot of new lovers.

And she tasted so good. Her mouth was hot and sweet and soft, and the lush curve of her lips fitted into his exactly like the pieces of a jigsaw. Holding his breath, he pulled her closer, kissing her back, gently teasing her lips apart with his tongue, pushing, probing, tasting her excitement, her hunger.

He heard her take a quick breath, like a gasp, almost as if she was drowning, and then she was swaying forward, her slender body pressing into the wall of his chest. He let go of the jacket and cupped her face with his hands, angling her head for a better fit. He deepened the kiss, back and forth, deeper and deeper, losing himself in the raggedness of her breath and the feel of her fingers biting into his arms.

It was as if all the jagged edges between them had softened. Everything was smooth and easy. And he was nothing but a man. A man who knew the rhythm of her body...the beat of her heart. All of her was close and warm—and his.

Letting his mouth slip down the pale arc of her throat, he felt his body grow harder as she moaned softly. And then her hands were in his hair, tangling, tightening, holding him captive, pulling him closer so that he almost lost his footing.

His heart running wild, he nudged her back towards the sofa, his knee between her thighs, and lowered her onto the cushions, his mouth still fused with hers, his hands moving beneath her body, lifting her closer, pressing her soft belly against the hardness of his erection.

Her dress had fallen away from her shoulder and he kissed the skin there, breathing in the scent of her beneath the perfume. Then he traced a path with his tongue to the soft mound of her breast, tugging the lacy bra aside to suck the stiff peak of her nipple into his mouth.

As she swallowed, deep in her throat, tiny shivers of fire and need darted over his skin and he groaned softly, lifting his face and moving lower to kiss the soft skin of her stomach, then lower still...

She arched against him, moving frantically and pulling at his shirt, her mouth seeking his blindly. And then he felt her hand press against the outline of his erection, and he was arching against her, his breath jerking. Her fingers were pulling at his waistband and, pulse quickening, he reached to help her, his hunger rolling through him like wildfire. He was close to losing control...

'And you know how easy it is to lose one's head in the heat of the moment.' Oscar's voice was soft inside his head. *'Things got out of hand. It wasn't intentional. She's mortified.'*

His body stilled, muscles tensing, and he shook his head as if that might expel Oscar's malicious drawl. But he could still hear it, whispering at the margins of his mind, like a prompter in the wings.

'Things got out of hand... She's mortified.'

'What is it?'

Dove was gazing up at him, her grey eyes huge and dazed, her mouth pinkly swollen from his feverish kisses.

'Gabriel?'

Gritting his teeth, ignoring the huskiness in her voice and the protests of his body, he peeled himself away from the treacherous heat of her skin and got to his feet.

Breathing shakily, Dove stared at him in confusion. Her head was swimming, her body pulsing uncontrollably, her skin burning from the heat of his touch.

But Gabriel was no longer touching her.

He was standing with his back to her, and that in itself should have been a red flag.

But she wasn't thinking straight. Glancing down at her dishevelled state, she felt her shoulders stiffen. Actually, her brain hadn't been involved at all.

'We should call it a night.'

She stared at his back, felt his words bouncing into one another inside her head, as random and ridiculous as bumper cars at a funfair.

'Call it a night…?' she echoed.

As he turned to face her, her skin jumped as if he'd touched her.

'We start early tomorrow, and as this acquisition is so important to both of us it would be better if there are no distractions.'

Around her the sea and sky seemed to have merged, so that it felt as if she was surrounded by a never-ending darkness that was keeping everything else at bay.

'And that's what this was? A distraction.'

But how could that be true? It wasn't possible to kiss someone like that—as if the world was about to end—and then just lose interest and walk away. Her heart felt as if it was in a vice. What was she talking about? She knew it was possible, and true, because Gabriel had done exactly that six years ago.

And now she had allowed him to do it all over again.

The realisation pierced her, slicing so deeply she felt as if she might double up.

'After what happened in London it was clear to me that we both had something we needed to work out of our systems…' He paused, and his blue gaze rested on her face, cool and distant as the exosphere. 'And now we have. So, yes, this was a distraction. A necessary one. Because now we can concentrate on the job in hand. That's what matters here.'

'That's what matters...' she repeated slowly, trying to square his words, the remoteness in his voice and the rigidity in his spine with the hot-mouthed lover of moments earlier.

He stared down at her. 'I'm not saying it wasn't enjoyable in the short term. But that's the point of a distraction. It's not the main event. It doesn't matter enough to last. I would have thought you of all people could understand that. Try not to take it personally, Dove. It's just business. It always was—although maybe you didn't understand that.'

She surged to her feet, swaying slightly as she clutched her dress around her trembling body. This was the man who had broken her heart all those years ago. The man who had ruthlessly blackmailed her into working for him to punish her for revealing his worst self to the world.

'You're contradicting yourself, Gabriel. You're the one who said this was personal.'

Her face felt hot, and she was acutely conscious of how she must look, with her hair spilling onto her shoulders and her dress gaping at the front, but she was too angry to care. Too shocked and horrified by how close she had come to letting her hunger take her back to the past.

'But I guess that's how you live with yourself, isn't it?' she said. 'By twisting and distorting things to fit your purpose—'

'I didn't twist anything.' His face was like stone, the high, flat cheekbones a cliff face of contempt, and his words were like hard little chips of rock. 'You just don't like having to accept responsibility for your behaviour.'

They were facing each other, their bodies straining, their anger circling them, pushing them closer like a fang-toothed creature.

'*My* behaviour?' She said the word slowly, not quite able to believe what she was hearing. Her lungs felt as if they were on fire. 'I'm not the guilty party here, Gabriel.'

'Why? Because you sent your snobbish father to do your dirty work? You're such a hypocrite.'

'And you're a fraud.'

'At least I own my mistakes.'

'If by "mistake" you mean our relationship, then you didn't own anything. You sneaked away like the coward you are.'

'Except I'm not the one who sent Daddy to make my excuses.'

'I didn't send anyone!' she snapped.

He was shaking his head. 'Sent. Asked. Coaxed. What's the difference? You're just trying to shift the blame.'

'I know exactly who's to blame.' The injustice of his words clawed at her soul. '*You* took a bribe. *You* took my father's money.'

'And what? You think you were worth more?'

His voice scraped over her skin like a serrated

knife and she heard her breath escape in a tiny, ragged gasp. Suddenly she felt as if she might throw up. A flare of anger exploded inside her, white and hot and so bright it could have lit up the night sky.

'I could ask you the same question. After all, you're the one who got paid off, Gabriel—not me. You're the one who put a value on our relationship and your part in it.'

His expression didn't alter, but when he spoke she could hear the rage in his voice, feel it rolling towards her in waves.

'But I didn't have a part in it—did I, Dove?'

Their eyes met—hers shocked, his blazing with fury, and a pain that took her breath and her anger away. But before she had a chance to respond, a chance to ask him what he meant, he turned and walked swiftly off the deck.

Heart pounding, she stared after him. Her head felt as if it had been punched. After the sound and fury of moments earlier the deck felt preternaturally quiet and still, like a stage after the curtain had fallen and everyone had left the theatre.

Everyone but her.

She was still there…alone, abandoned, again.

Her legs started to shake uncontrollably and she sank down onto the sofa. Beside her, his jacket lay discarded against the cushions, and she had to fight an urge to pick it up and hold it close.

Beyond the pale wood the sea was dark and

smooth. A black mirror that swallowed up ships and secrets. Including, she realised with a jolt of misery, those of the man who had just stormed off the deck.

CHAPTER FIVE

'COFFEE?'

'Thanks, Chris.'

Looking up from her laptop, Dove smiled as she took the cup from the lanky analyst. She liked Chris. He was polite, helpful, disciplined and focused. Like everyone on the Silva team he was good at his job. But, as in all well-run businesses, the staff took their lead from the top—and Gabriel was a remarkable boss.

Glancing over to where he was talking on the phone, at the edge of the room, his profile carving a pure gold line against the background of glittering blue, she felt her stomach knot. She had been working on the acquisition for five days now, but it had become obvious to her after less than five minutes why Gabriel Silva had achieved such stratospheric success.

He was not just smart, but also clear-minded. He made everything seem simple, at the same time acknowledging the shifts and fluctuations that would inevitably complicate the process. In the same way, he knew what he wanted from every member of his team.

Her cheeks felt warm.

One thing was clear. His staff didn't need to be blackmailed into working for him. In fact, it was quite likely that they would have worked for him for free.

None of the seven women and five men sitting around the huge lacquered white table had a bad word to say about their boss and most of them had a lot of good—offering up stories, unprompted, of how Gabriel had supported and empowered them in some way.

And she believed them. Even to a critical observer like herself it was obvious that he encouraged his staff to be independent, self-motivated, and to take pride in what they did. And it worked. The entire team was as invested in this acquisition as he was.

All except her.

She hadn't shared her confusion, but privately she was surprised by Gabriel's determination to acquire Fairlight Holdings. It just didn't seem to match the pattern of his other acquisitions. But then if she could understand what drove Gabriel Silva to behave as he did, she wouldn't be sitting here...

'So, are there any other updates?' Gabriel was leaning forward now, over his laptop, typing something on the keyboard. He stepped back, his blue eyes scanning the room like a Roman emperor looking over the senate house.

She shifted in her seat so that she was shielded from his gaze by her neighbour.

'No? Then let's break for ten minutes.'

They all worked long hours, and sometimes at quiet points in the day she would notice him staring out to sea intently. At first, she'd thought he was just looking at the view. But there was always a tension in his body…almost as if he was looking for something. Something that wasn't there or that was just beyond the horizon.

In those moments she caught a glimpse of the serious young man she'd met six years ago. But then the next moment she would look again and see a stranger. A beautiful, intense stranger. Someone she had loved but never really known.

But was that even possible? To love someone and yet not know anything about them?

Apparently so—because what had she really known about Gabriel aside from his name and the fact that he was a waiter?

They had talked cautiously at first, in the way that all couples did at the beginning of a relationship. But they'd been young, and the air had been warm and honeyed, and most of that long hot summer had been spent in bed. They'd touched, slept, watched TV and each other, lying there and listening to the sound of each other's breathing.

And they'd had sex.

Teasing sex. Tender sex. Fierce sex, tearing at each other's clothes. Sex that had left them both clinging to one another as if they were drowning.

Her pulse fluttered. And last night they would have had sex on the deck if Gabriel hadn't stopped them.

Picking up her coffee with a hand that shook slightly, she took a sip. 'Ouch!' She jerked the cup away from her mouth. It was scalding hot.

'Are you okay?' Chris was leaning forward, his forehead creasing in concern.

'It's fine.' She smiled reassuringly. 'It's my own fault. I normally add milk, but I forgot.'

As she pressed her finger against her top lip she felt a cool shiver shoot down her spine and, glancing up, felt her insides tighten. Gabriel was watching her, his body taut and still like a stalking leopard, his blue eyes fixed on her mouth. Her heart thudded hard as he lifted his gaze, and for a moment they stared at each other across the room. Then abruptly he turned away to talk to Carrie Naylor.

His glance had been brief—a few seconds at most—but it had felt as intimate and tangible as a caress.

Breath snarling in her throat, she stared at his back, wishing she could shut her eyes and shut him out. But she knew from the last four restless nights that it wouldn't matter if she did. Asleep or awake, eyes open or shut, in daylight or darkness, she could always see Gabriel.

Even if she couldn't touch him.

Her fingers twitched against the keys of her laptop and she slid her hands into her lap, pressing them between her knees as if she didn't trust them. *Because she didn't.* She was like an addict. She might have spent six years sober, but when Gabriel had kissed her in London she'd been no more able to stop at one kiss than an alcoholic could stop at one drink.

Keeping her gaze fixed on the screen, she thought *again* about what had happened that night they'd been alone on deck. It had been reckless. Stupid. Dangerous. And yet despite being all those things it had felt like coming home.

There must be something wrong with her head— something wrong with *her*—to think that way after what he'd said to her, the way he'd acted. He had been cold, and cruel, and yet it wasn't his cruelty or his fury that was imprinted on her brain. It was that look on his face and the words he'd flung at her in response to the accusations she'd made about the part he'd played in their relationship.

'But I didn't have a part in it—did I, Dove?'

Her stomach tightened. When she wasn't replaying their heated on-deck encounter, she kept on trying unsuccessfully to untangle the meaning of those words as they rolled around inside her head.

But they still made absolutely no sense.

And it would probably stay that way.

It wasn't as if she could ask him, she thought,

glancing furtively to where he was now once more talking on the phone.

They hadn't been alone since that night on the deck. Gabriel's team had arrived early the following morning, and from that moment onwards there had been no opportunity to talk—much less kiss.

Breathing out a little unsteadily, she pressed her finger harder against her lip, replaying those endless seconds when the world had stopped moving,

'I thought this might help.'

She blinked. Chris was back.

'I got you some ice.' He held out a glass.

'Actually, applying ice to a burn is the worst thing you can do.'

A lean hand plucked the glass from her fingers and, her heart thumping in her chest, she looked up to find Gabriel standing beside her.

Every nerve in her body snapped onto high alert. Panic was snaking through her body—and something else…something that made her feel jittery and irritable.

'I know it feels logical, but it can cause further damage to the skin. Something to do with shutting off the capillaries too forcefully, I believe,' he said, in that quiet way of his that made her stomach knot. 'The best treatment is a cool compress.' He turned towards the analyst. 'Chris, could you go and ask one of the stewards to sort that out asap? Any of them will be able to help.'

In the moment of silence following the analyst's

departure his eyes found hers. She knew it shouldn't move her the way it did, like flame and chaos beneath her skin, but what should and shouldn't happen rarely seemed to be relevant where Gabriel was concerned.

'You didn't need to do that. It's really not a big deal,' she said stiffly, keeping her gaze firmly away from the man taking up too much space beside her.

'I'm afraid that's not your decision to make, Ms Cavendish.' His voice wrapped around her skin, as cool as the compress he'd suggested. 'You're on my yacht, so I'm responsible for your wellbeing. I wouldn't want Alistair thinking I don't take care of his people.'

Gabriel's people were all around them—typing, talking, taking notes—but it didn't matter. She could feel her body reacting just as if it were the two of them alone, her skin tingling and growing tighter, hotter.

The goosebumps of the other night had returned. She wanted to cover her arms, conceal her response, but that would only draw attention to the thing she was trying to hide. If only she could snatch the glass from his hand and upend the ice over her head and her overheated body.

Instead, she gave him a small, tight smile and said, with a briskness she'd perfected over the last five days, 'I'm sure Chris can look after me.' Still smiling stiffly, she glanced pointedly to the other end of the room, where the stewards had appeared with trays of freshly baked pastries. 'Don't let me keep you—'

She let the sentence teeter and balance in the space between them, but he didn't move away. He just stood there, staring down at her in that edgy, nerve-jangling, quiet way of his.

'You work hard,' he said finally.

It wasn't what she was expecting him to say, but it was business, not personal, she told herself. And yet the glitter in his eyes didn't feel impersonal.

By now most of the team had gravitated towards the burnished pastries at the end of the room and she refocused her gaze, away from Gabriel's distracting face to where the Mediterranean sparkled in the midday sun. Only that was like looking straight into his glittering blue eyes…

'Did you think I wouldn't? I'm not that petty,' she said, answering her own question.

She *was* working hard—but not because of the threats he'd made back in London, if that was what he was implying. For her, there was something intensely satisfying about helping a complex, multitiered business acquire another.

Lifting her chin, she looked past his shoulder at the door, wishing she was on the other side of it. And that it was locked and barred and guarded by a couple of large, unfriendly dogs.

'And, just for the record, my work ethic has nothing to do with your "incentive" either. Believe it or not, you're not the most difficult or demanding client I've ever worked for.'

For a moment Gabriel didn't reply. She tried to pretend that his silence didn't get to her, but eventually she couldn't help herself, and she looked up to find him watching her intently, as if she was a puzzle he was trying to work out.

'I don't know whether to be disappointed or flattered.'

That remark was accompanied by a small, crooked smile that made a flicker of heat fan out low in her pelvis.

Their eyes locked. 'I should stick with disappointed,' she said, her arm curved across her stomach to press against the ache that still lingered there from when Gabriel had kissed her five days ago. 'That way you won't have to go out of your comfort zone.'

There was a beat of silence. His face was unreadable, but his blue gaze seemed to tear into her.

'I wasn't the one who was disappointed,' he replied.

She stared at him, struggling to breathe, as if his cryptic words had displaced all the air in the room. That was the second, or maybe the third time he had insinuated that *she* was the guilty party in their relationship.

'You know, if you have something to say—'

'Here we are.'

Chris was back again. This time, he was holding a compress and a bowl of presumably cool water.

'Sorry I took so long. I got confused on the way back and went left instead of right.' Frowning, he glanced up at his boss. 'Sorry, did I interrupt something?'

Gabriel shook his head, his gaze beating down on her like a wave breaking. 'Not at all. Ms Cavendish and I are finished.'

It was lunchtime. Pushing his fork into the carefully arranged Cobb salad on his plate, Gabriel speared another piece of chicken. It was perfectly cooked, but he wasn't hungry.

Understandably, he thought, tilting back his head to gaze up at a melting yellow sun. But, much as he longed to do so, he knew he couldn't blame the heat of the day for his lack of appetite. Or for the tension that was making his body feel as if it might fly apart at any moment.

At the other end of the table he heard Dove laugh and his head turned without permission, drawn irresistibly to the sound, and to the pale curve of her throat.

Not that he needed to look to know where she was. For the last five days he had been devastatingly aware of her exact position in any room, and his neck and shoulders ached with the effort of not looking at her.

He gritted his teeth.

And his body ached with the effort of not crossing the room and finishing what she had started on the deck five days ago. Fortunately the constant presence of one or other member of his team had acted as an unwitting chaperone, so that his feverish imaginings had stayed in his imagination.

But even though he had kept his distance he couldn't avoid Dove completely, and whichever way he turned it felt as if she was always there, poised and polished, with her pale blonde hair smoothly knotted at the nape of her neck.

Turn left and she was leaning forward to look at some paperwork, her bottom pushing against the fabric of one of those snug-fitting pencil skirts that seemed designed to make him unravel.

Turn right and she was biting into the soft pink cushion of her lower lip as she talked on the phone.

Occasionally, when required to do so, she would meet his gaze, with a cool, defensive light in her grey eyes.

Glancing down the table, he felt his stomach twist. And now she was laughing with someone other than him, her eyes dancing with light and delight.

It made him want to punch something.

His jaw was so tight it felt as if it had been wired together. He had made himself wait so long to get to this moment of reckoning, but things weren't going quite how he'd imagined they would.

Forcing Dove to work for him, taking her out of her comfort zone, was supposed to punish her—but instead he felt as if he was the one being punished. And, rather than confirming that she was a heartless bitch who had used and then discarded him, he kept seeing her pale, stunned face as she'd tried to cover her body.

Putting down his fork, he gave up pretending to eat and picked up his water glass instead. Although frankly he would rather it was wine. Or better still whisky. Then at least he could numb his senses and dull the ache of need.

But why was he putting himself through this? He had made his point in bringing her here. There was no need to extend this torture any more. He could dismiss her as she had dismissed him. Although, unlike Dove and Fenella, he would do it in person.

Thinking about Fenella made his stomach knot. When he'd found out that she was looking to sell the family firm, it seemed like fate. Finally a chance to do something concrete that would make it impossible for her to ignore him. With the added bonus of his being able to pay her off.

It was a convoluted way to prove a point, and it certainly wasn't good business—Alistair Cox had been right about that. There were many other, better property companies. But that was part of it. He wanted to show her that she had been wrong to give him away. That unlike the son she had kept, he was a business leader who had so much money he could afford to waste it in acquiring her precious family firm. The family that *he* had no part of.

But first he would deal with Dove.

He waited until lunch was over and his team were back around the table.

'Before we begin, I want to thank everyone for their hard work. As usual, your focus and dedication has been outstanding. Please know that it is recognised and greatly appreciated.'

He paused. Now that the moment was here, he felt an uncharacteristic flicker of doubt.

And that was why he needed to end this now, he thought irritably. Dove did something to him that no one else did. She made him feel things, want things. She confused him…

Remembering how her body had curved against his, he felt his groin harden. But she wasn't just making him unravel physically. He was so tense right now, and he'd reached for her because she was still the only person alive who could soothe him. Only that had angered him, and that was why he'd lost his temper with her. Said things that he should have kept hidden. And since that night more things, more feelings, had kept slipping out.

He was like a wound seeping blood. And he couldn't risk haemorrhaging any more ugly, sordid truths about himself. Certainly not to Dove.

'We now have several valuation models for the target company, and sufficient information to enable us to construct a reasonable offer, so today will be our last day here together. We'll wrap things up tonight and start back again on Monday morning in London. Sorry, people,'

There were a few groans, followed by applause. Then several members of his team came over to him, and it was a couple of minutes before he could look over to where Dove was sitting.

She was staring down at her laptop, but as if sensing his gaze she looked up at him, and he felt his pulse stumble.

He had expected her to look relieved, but instead her grey eyes were the colour of storm clouds.

Leaning back against the lounger, Gabriel gazed out to sea. It was only nine o'clock and the sun was starting to rise through the clear blue sky. The day was just beginning.

Normally there would be a background hum of people talking and laughing as they opened laptops and shuffled papers. But not this morning. This morning there was no sound aside from the gentle slap of water against the boat. He was alone. The day was his. He could change out of his work clothes and take a dip in the pool, laze in the sun, maybe finish that book he'd started six months ago. He could have a drink—a cocktail, perhaps. A Last Word might be apt…particularly if he got the stewards to go heavy on the gin.

His team had left after an early breakfast.

And Dove had gone with them.

His jaw tightened. She had shaken his hand before she'd left and said goodbye in that careful, precise way of hers. Remembering the cool touch of her fingers, he felt his throat tighten. It had all been very polite, very civilised. Maybe that was why he felt so dissatisfied now. So thwarted.

Swearing softly, he got to his feet and stalked to the other side of the deck—only to remember as he got there that he was standing where Dove had reached up and kissed him. For a second the air around him seemed to ripple and, his heart beating out of time, he scowled down at the smooth teak.

Did events imprint themselves on buildings? He closed his eyes. Could wood and brick retain some memory of the heat and intensity of human encounters?

He breathed in deeply, then tensed. He could almost smell her scent…that teasing light mix of summertime and sweet peas. His eyes snapped open and he blinked into the sunlight. And now he was seeing her. Holding his breath, he gazed across the deck at the blurred shape of a woman. Except, of course, it wasn't her. It was just a mirage. An illusion caused by the refraction of light off the gleaming polished deck.

The shape moved and everything inside him slid sideways, almost as if the yacht had run aground. But it wasn't *The Argentum* that had run aground. It was him.

And the woman standing on the other side of the deck wasn't a mirage.

Something swift and sharp scudded across his skin and he watched in stunned, silent disbelief, his mind groping for some kind of explanation, as Dove Cavendish walked slowly towards him.

She had changed clothes. The clinging pencil skirt and soft blouse were gone. Instead she was wearing denim shorts and one of those blue and white striped matelot tops, and her hair was tied loosely at the nape of her neck.

His hands flexed by his sides as she stopped about a yard away. She looked nervous, but defiant—and shatteringly beautiful.

None of which helped explain why she was still on board his yacht...

His head was starting to spin and he realised that he was still holding his breath. He let it out carefully and, hoping that he looked more composed than he felt, he said softly, 'What the hell are you doing here?'

That was a good question, Dove thought as she felt her stomach drop to her feet. One to which she should probably have a ready-made answer. But earlier, when she'd been sneaking back to her cabin, she hadn't given much thought as to what she would say when she finally confronted Gabriel. She'd been too busy worrying that she would get caught.

There had been no plan. It had been a spur-of-the-moment decision—the kind her mother had warned her about. The kind she knew led to heartbreak and despair. So of course she had ignored the warnings.

Now, though, she wished she had come prepared. It was hard to breathe, much less string a sentence together, when he was standing there with the fading sun's rays caressing his beautiful face like a lover. And he did look particularly beautiful. Beautiful and formidable...

But she couldn't say for sure whether it was his beauty or his severity that was making her pulse dance a tarantella across her skin.

'We have things to sort out...things we need to talk about—'

'Such dedication,' he said, cutting her off. 'But I think it can wait until Monday, don't you?'

She took a deep breath. 'It's not about the acquisition.'

'Then there's nothing to talk about,' he said, in that soft, lethal way of his that made her want to dive into the Mediterranean. And made her body shiver in response.

Tilting her chin, she met his gaze. 'How can you say that after what happened the other night?'

His eyes narrowed. 'I'm saying it *because* of the other night.' Shaking his head, he turned. 'Go home, Ms Cavendish.'

Anger rose up like a wave, swallowing her whole. Moving swiftly, she stepped in front of him. 'I am so done with you turning your back on me. Being rich doesn't give you the right to be rude, you know?'

'Actually, it does,' he said softly. 'It pretty much gives you licence to do whatever you damn well like. Like bribing someone to get out of your life, for example.'

She stared at him, her pulse beating so fast she thought she would pass out. 'That's not the same.'

'Of course it isn't.'

'You're twisting things again—'

'No, everything is plumb-straight.' He stared down at her, his face taut. 'Go home, Dove. You have work on Monday—an acquisition to close. That's all that matters here.'

She shook her head. 'Then you're going to have to fire me and get someone else, because I am not leaving this boat until we've had a conversation.'

There: she had a plan, after all. And she would do it. She would chain herself to the ship's wheel if she had to.

There was a tiny snatch of air around them.

'And it's always about what *you* want, isn't it?' His voice was harder and edgier than before. It sounded like bones snapping. 'When to talk. When to end things.'

For a moment she couldn't breathe. His words thudded inside her head in a terrifying drumroll. 'That's not true.' She tried to shake her head, as if that would somehow validate her denial, but her head wouldn't move. 'I didn't end anything. *You* ended us.'

'Is that what you tell yourself? Tell other people?'

'No, it's what happened. My father offered you money and you took it.'

Her pulse jerked as he took a step closer, his blue eyes sharpening on her face.

'And you can't complain about that. Not when you made sure that was all that was on offer.'

Her hand crept up to her throat and she stared at him, mute with shock. She had offered him so much more than that. And he had tossed it aside.

'That had nothing to do with me. My father went to see you because he didn't trust you. He didn't think you were who you said you were.'

Gabriel's face stilled. 'What do you mean?'

'He thought you were a gold-digger. A chancer.' Remembering how she had defended him to her father, she felt her face burn. 'So he went to the hotel to find you. To test you. And you failed.'

She saw his jaw tighten.

'You set me up to fail.'

His tone was still harsh, but now there was a different note beneath the anger and frustration, almost questioning, as if he was asking her, not telling her.

'Of course I didn't.' Her head was spinning. 'Why would I do that?'

I loved you, she finished silently. Hadn't he known that? Hadn't he known how much she'd loved him?

Gabriel was staring past her, almost as if he had forgotten she was there. 'That's what I've been asking myself for six years.'

Her heart was beating slow and heavy, as if it was

being squeezed in a fist. Something wasn't right. At the margins of her mind pictures were forming, then blurring too fast for her to follow them.

She took a painful shallow breath, then another. 'Well, you're not the only one with unanswered questions, Gabriel,' she said hoarsely. 'So why don't we answer them once and for all? Why don't we say what has to be said, and then we can get on with our lives? That's what you want, isn't it?'

It was why she was standing there. Why she had stayed on *The Argentum*. But when finally he turned to look at her and nodded, his blue eyes darker than she had ever seen before, she felt no relief—just a shattering sense of sadness.

CHAPTER SIX

IT WAS THE QUICK, easy rhythm of the stewards' voices, so similar they were almost interchangeable, that grabbed Dove's attention.

Not that she was really reading. The book in her hands was just a prop. Something to stop her from staring at the man sitting on the other side of the cabin or thinking about what she had set in motion. Up until that moment it had certainly helped with the former. The latter, not so much. Pretty much from the moment Gabriel's private jet had taken off in Nice her brain had been preoccupied with all the possible outcomes after it landed.

Her heart beat hard and slow as the stewards walked back up the cabin, smiling politely as they passed. They were friends as well as colleagues—she could tell. That was why they sounded so alike. She had read about it in a magazine at the hairdresser's. It was called phonetic convergence, and it was something that happened between close friends and family. She had it with her mother.

But with Gabriel that mirroring and overlapping had only ever happened with their bodies. When they'd talked he'd been guarded, careful, and there had always been a point in any conversation where he'd checked himself.

When they'd talked.

It was ironic that since agreeing to talk to her on the deck of *The Argentum* Gabriel had said approximately twenty words to her. Maybe he thought that the cabin of a plane—even a spacious private jet like this one—was not private enough for the conversation they needed to have.

But then they could have stayed on the yacht.

Turning her head slightly, she gazed down through the oval of glass at the water below. They had been in the air for nearly four hours, en route to Pico, one of the islands of the Azores off the coast of Portugal, where Gabriel owned the Quinta dos Louros—a private estate and vineyard.

She had thought they were going back to London. It had only been when they were taking off that he had told her they were flying to Pico. He'd given her no explanation, and she'd been so stunned that he had agreed to talk that it hadn't occurred to her to argue or cross-examine him. Later, when the burn of adrenalin had faded, she'd concluded that it was just his way of regaining the upper hand and put it to the back of her mind.

Her throat tightened. But now other things were taking centre stage—specifically Gabriel's insistence that it was she who had sent her father to end things on her behalf. The anger and pain on his face was bright and achingly clear in her memory.

Her eyes darted to where he sat, working on his laptop, his long legs taking up every inch of the generous space in front of his seat.

It wasn't the first time Gabriel had accused her of sending her father to end their relationship, but she hadn't given it much thought before. It had felt more like a question of semantics, not fact. He had as good as said so himself.

'Sent. Asked. Coaxed. What's the difference? You're just trying to shift the blame.'

They were his words, but they could just as easily apply to her. She'd assumed he was trying to shift the blame—lying to her, and to himself, because he didn't want to associate the billionaire businessman he saw every day in the mirror with the greedy, unscrupulous, self-serving man he had been six years ago.

She felt her heartbeat catch.

But yesterday it had been clear from the unfiltered rawness in his voice and the tense way he'd held his body that Gabriel believed what he was saying. He really did think that it had been her idea. That, in his words, she had sent her 'snobbish father' to do her dirty work.

Only what had she ever done to make him think that she was that kind of person?

Suddenly afraid that he might look over and answer her question, she turned and stared out of the window at the silvery blue water. A drumroll of nervousness hammered across her skin. There had been nothing but ocean for hours. But now she could see shapes appearing in the distance. Vast, jagged outcrops of rock splashed with vivid green, were rising out of the Atlantic like the spine of some huge prehistoric creature. She was looking at the Azores.

The plane landed fifteen minutes later. From the air the archipelago had looked dark, almost menacing, but as she stepped out of the plane into the pale morning light she felt her mouth drop. There was only one word that could describe what she was seeing: epic.

Everywhere was green and lush and humming with sound and life. What wasn't green was black, and towering above the landscape was a mountain crowned in wispy clouds.

'It's called Montanho di Pico, which means mountain peak.'

She jumped as Gabriel's voice cut across her thoughts.

'It's where the island got its name,' he said. 'Although it's more than just a mountain—it's also a volcano.'

A volcano.

Her chin jerked up towards the towering peak. Back on the boat, she'd thought they had called a truce. So naturally he'd brought her to an island which could be covered in hot lava at any moment.

'I did wonder why we couldn't just talk on the yacht,' she said, her eyes narrowing on the distant summit. 'Now it's all starting to make more sense. Although I have to say it does feel a little contrived. I mean, we were in the middle of the Mediterranean. You could have just made me walk the plank if you wanted to do away with me.'

There was a small silence. She caught a sharp glint of blue as he turned his head. 'Unfortunately I didn't have one on hand. It was on the list of optional extras, but I chose a submersible and a jet ski instead.'

Their eyes met and the intimacy of years earlier branched out, blossoming effortlessly, just like it had on the deck of *The Argentum*. She felt her heart thud inside her chest and wondered what would happen if she took his hand and told him that she didn't want to talk any more. That there were other things they did better.

And then his eyes flicked away, and she wondered if she was losing her mind.

'Seriously, you don't need to worry. It's what's known as a quiescent volcano. That means it's not active, but it's still registering seismic activity.'

A bit like the man standing beside her, she thought, remembering that ripple of deep anger beneath the flare of frustration and resentment. Which made her either stupid or unhinged. After all, what kind of person went anywhere near a volcano, quiescent or not?

He guided her towards the stocky off-road vehicle that sat at the edge of the runway. As they walked towards the waiting car his fingers brushed against hers and she felt her skin pop, but if Gabriel noticed he gave no sign.

There was no traffic on the road, and soon they were climbing into the green hills. But it didn't seem to matter how high or in which direction they went, the mountain still cast its vast triangular shadow across them.

For the next twenty minutes she forgot everything but the view from her window. Up close, the landscape looked almost extra-terrestrial, with its rippling outcrops of long-since cooled black magma. Then they swept round a corner and there was a crater-shaped lake, edged with swathes of delicate ferns the colour of parakeets and strange-looking trees with swollen, crepey trunks. She felt her heartbeat accelerate. It was the first time she'd had a sense of what the planet might have looked like before humans had begun to dominate it.

'They're called dragon trees.'

She frowned. 'Is that because their trunks look like dragon's legs?'

'Good guess...'

His eyes rested on her face and she felt the darkness in the pupils shudder all the way through her.

'But I'm afraid the truth is a little more far-fetched—as is often the case. Supposedly they got their name when Hercules killed the hundred-headed dragon guarding the garden of the Hesperides. Everywhere the blood spilled a dragon tree grew. Or so the myth goes.'

Hearing him speak, she felt that same dark magnetic pull as earlier. It was no wonder she had fallen for him. Fallen for his stories. This was a man who could make a tree sound sexy. And she was here with him, on a clump of volcanic rock, with nothing but hundreds of miles of sea in every direction. And there was nothing she could do about that now.

The road gave a tiny, sharp twist to the left and she felt the car slow. It was too late to do anything. They had arrived.

She stared in silence at the rugged grey stone house in front of her. Oaklands, her childhood home, was beautiful, but like most big country houses in England it was designed to be the jewel in the crown of its parkland setting. This house was different. It looked as if it had been birthed from the land, with the mountain soaring into the clouds behind and in front the wild green curves of vegetation tilting away to the Atlantic.

Inside, the Quinta dos Louros had little in common with Oaklands' chintzy, antique-filled interior. Someone—possibly Gabriel, more likely some expensive designer—had decided to let the scale of the rooms and the light seeping in from the ocean speak for itself, and the result was a masterclass in sophisticated simplicity that was as beautiful and cool as its owner.

His housekeeper was waiting in the hall, and after a quick meet-and-greet—her name was Sara—Gabriel took her on a brief tour of the house, including her bedroom. Finally, he led her back downstairs into a sitting room the size of a tennis court.

She turned a slow, admiring three-hundred-and-sixty-degree circle. 'It's amazing,' she said truthfully.

Everything felt balanced, calm and comfortable, so that she had the oddest feeling—almost as if she had come home. Although she had never once felt like that walking into Oaklands, she thought with a jolt. There was always an edge inside her whenever she went home—a pulse-skipping apprehension about whether she would find Oscar and Olivia sniping at each other over the dining table or her mother weeping alone in her bedroom.

Just thinking about it made her spine snap to attention. She'd hated everything about those rows. The weave of tension beforehand. The sickly swell as the accusations and counter accusations had started, building to the actual row itself. Mostly pointless. Often vicious. Always exhausting. And then, the worst part of all, the terrible aftermath when all the things that shouldn't have been said lingered in the shadows.

Now, as her eyes flicked to the sunlit corners of the room, she realised that she had no idea how long she had been standing there in silence, and that Ga-

briel was staring at her, the blue in his gaze bright
and sharp in a way that made it hard to breathe.

'Take a seat,' he said finally. 'I've asked Sara to
bring us some coffee.'

Gabriel waited until Dove had sat down on one of
the pale green linen sofas, then dropped into his favourite armchair—the one which offered up an uninterrupted view of the Atlantic. But today his eyes
were resting on Dove's face, because even an ink-
coloured ocean that covered twenty percent of the
earth's surface seemed to fade into insignificance
beside her pearlescent beauty.

She looked tired and on edge, he thought. A week
ago that would have pleased him immensely. But a
week was a long time in business—particularly, it
turned out, when you were working with the woman
who had broken your heart. Long enough for the
countless things he had taken for granted to become
not quite so cut and dried.

Some, he'd discovered, were simply not true. Having worked alongside her for five days, he knew now
that she wasn't the talentless, entitled heiress to the
family firm he'd imagined her to be. She was diligent, disciplined, and good at her job. In another
lifetime he wouldn't have hesitated to offer her a job
with the Silva Group.

But it was the past—their past—that seemed to
be shifting before his eyes like the shards of mir-

ror and glass in a kaleidoscope. Only how was that even possible? The past was history. Unchangeable, fixed, immutable.

And yet this morning he'd felt himself waver. Just for a moment he'd let her get inside his head, and for a few half-seconds he had questioned what he knew to be true. Even questioned himself. That was why he had agreed to talk to her—so that he could pin her down, refute every single one of her lies and exorcise her from his blood once and for all.

Of course, that didn't explain why he'd needed to bring her all the way here.

Gritting his teeth, he ignored that little voice inside his head, just as he ignored the flicker of heat that danced across his skin every time she walked in or out of a room. Every day he was ignoring more and more. Soon he would be like one of those sightless creatures that lived in the darkness of the Mariana Trench.

Thankfully Sara arrived at that moment, with coffee and some delicate lacy biscuits. After she'd left, closing the door softly, he leaned back in his chair.

Now what?

He felt stretched taut. There was no process for this. He had no idea how to start the conversation he wanted to have. Or even if he wanted to have it. It would mean reliving the moment of her rejection by proxy that had sent him spinning into the darkness...

'Why did you choose to buy a house on Pico? Is there some family connection?'

Dove's voice cut through his thoughts and he glanced over to where she was sitting. She was talking about his father. His adoptive father—Luis. But his biological father—the man who had spent a night with Fenella Ogilvy thirty years ago—was a man without a name or a face. Not 'hat he could tell her that. He couldn't tell anyone. But he especially couldn't tell Dove.

'No, not really.' He shook his head. 'My father's family come from Porto. But when I first went out to the States I made friends with some surfers. They were taking a trip to São Jorge and they invited me along.'

He saw her ball her hands into fists. So they had got there in the end. It had been by means of a rather circuitous route, but they were there nonetheless.

'Of course. You went surfing after we broke up.' Her mouth twisted. 'And there I was, worrying that your guilty conscience might be keeping you awake all night. Only how could it? You don't *have* a conscience.' She shook her head. 'You know, I keep thinking about what you said earlier. About *me* setting *you* up to fail. But it was you who set me up. You met me at that party and you thought, *Here's someone I can scam.*'

Wrong, he thought silently, his gaze roaming over her flushed cheeks and that lush pink mouth. When he'd met her at that party, he had thought she was every man's fantasy come to life. And he had wanted her. God, how he had wanted her. He still wanted her now, and he hated that…

'And you didn't think at all,' he said. 'You just took. Because you could.' They were both on the edge of their seats, fists clenched, eyes narrowed. 'Because you were rich and beautiful and bored.'

It was the way she had been brought up, he told himself, remembering Oscar Cavendish's cool, reptilian smile and his arrogant assumption that the world had been set up to satisfy his wishes above all others.

He held her gaze. 'That's how you people operate.'

'Which people?' She was staring at him, her grey eyes wide with confusion and an exhaustion he refused to acknowledge.

'You and your *friends*.' He tossed the word at her as if it was a grenade, and they both jerked to their feet at the same time. 'Those trust-fund babies who went to all those parties. The ones who used to get drunk and smash stuff up, and then just throw money on the table as if that made everything all right. You told me you were different.'

He had thought she *was* different. Gentle and sensitive. And the way she had looked at him then… There had almost been a purity to it.

'I was. I *am*,' she protested shakily.

At some point they had edged closer to one another, drawn by the invisible gravitational pull of desire, and now he could see the faint tremor beneath her skin, the flush across her cheeks. He wanted to touch her so much, and that knowledge made him furious.

'No, you're exactly the same. The only difference is you don't pay with cash,' he snarled.

For a splinter of a second she stared at him in the jagged silence that followed his remark, and then she took an unsteady step backwards.

'And that's the sticking point for you, isn't it? That's why you agreed to this.' A hard flare of anger crossed her face. 'You hate me knowing that you took the money. It makes you feel small. But frankly—and this might come as a shock to you, Gabriel—I don't care about your pride.'

Her face was pale and wide-eyed, but her voice had stopped shaking.

'I care about mine. So I'm going to get my bags, and then I'm getting off this island on the next boat or plane. In fact, I'll swim if I have to.'

She spun round and was gone, moving with a grace that his eyes tracked even in his feverish state, moving so swiftly she was already in her bedroom by the time he caught up with her. As he slammed the door shut behind them she stepped towards him, her eyes blazing.

'What do you think you're doing?'

And now his anger was blazing too—rolling through him high and fast, like a bushfire.

'You think I needed to bring you here to work out that you don't care about my pride? You left me sitting in that hotel bar for nearly four hours,' he said, and it cost him a lot to keep his voice calm, when the muted agony of it was still reverberating inside him. 'Do you know how humiliating that was?'

There was a pulsing silence, broken only by the fractured sound of their breathing.

'You want to talk about humiliation?' She lifted her chin like a boxer entering the ring—a flyweight squaring up to a heavyweight. 'Try coming in second place to a pile of money.'

Fire and fury swirled in her beautiful grey eyes along with something less sharp, something shadowy and frayed that almost undid him.

'You turned our relationship into a financial transaction.'

He stepped forward, his hands closing around the tops of her arms. 'No, you sent your father to do that, Dove.'

'For the last time—I didn't send him to find you and I never asked him to pay you off. I didn't know anything about what he'd done until he came and told me.'

She tried to pull away from him but he tightened his grip, holding her firmly, pressing his fingers into her skin.

'You're lying. How did he find me, then? No one knew about us except you and me.' He felt a sting of shame. 'You didn't want anyone to know. Or are you going to deny that too?'

He could tell from the heavy silence that followed his question that she wasn't, but instead of feeling a warm rush of satisfaction, he felt a dull ache creeping through his chest.

'There was no way your father could have found out where I was waiting unless you told him.'

'I didn't tell him.'

Now she jerked her arms violently, and this time he let her go. Her beautiful face was pale and the shake was back in her voice as she said, 'I don't know how he found out. But I do know that when he offered you money to leave me you took it.'

He stared down at her, his heart hammering against his ribs. She was making it sound so easy, and in some ways it had been. All he'd had to do was say yes. Only it was so much more complicated than that. More than anything he had wanted to throw the money back in Oscar's face, take his rage and his pain and unleash it upon the woman who couldn't even be bothered to reject him in person.

But confronting Dove, making her *feel* what she had done to him, would have meant revealing so much—too much. That was why he had taken the money and walked. Because the hardest thing to do had also been the easiest.

He shook his head. 'That's not how it happened.'

'Then tell me what did happen.'

Remembering the helpless, nightmarish daze of his conversation with Oscar Cavendish, he felt his stomach knot. But he knew they had always been heading to this point. Everything along the way had just been diversions on the road…

* * *

The train had been delayed twice. First because of engineering works, then because of a points failure. Gabriel checked his phone again. But he had left plenty of time, so he still had ten minutes to spare before Dove was due to meet him in the hotel bar, and they weren't flying out to the States until this evening.

The dingy hotel wouldn't have been his choice, he thought as he nodded at the barmaid. But Dove had suggested it, and it would only be for one drink.

He ordered a lager that he knew he was too nervous to drink and forced his breathing to slow. They had agreed to tell their parents after they'd reached California. Part of him would have liked to tell his family now; he knew they were worried about him, and that they would worry less when they met Dove.

Her parents would almost certainly be less enthusiastic about the match. She hadn't said as much, but he'd guessed that was why she wanted to keep their relationship a secret. And he understood secrets.

His phone buzzed and, picking it up, he felt his heart skip a beat as he read the message from Dove.

Running late. Wait for me.

She was never late—but then it wasn't every day you ran off with your lover.

He stared down at the screen, seeing Dove's soft

grey eyes, and that extraordinarily sweet smile that made his heart bang like a drum.

It had done more than that. Her smile, her love, had been a balm for the sting of Fenella's rejection. Dove made him feel safe and reckless. He almost wrote back *Until the end of time*... But in the end he settled for a simple X.

'Can I get you another drink?'

The barmaid was hovering by the table.

'Why not?' He held out his glass. 'And a gin and tonic as well, please.'

'Are you meeting someone?' Her face changed just a little.

He nodded. 'She's running a bit late.'

Just one drink.

Running a bit late.

Throughout the afternoon, as the minutes ticked into first one and then two and then three hours, he remembered those words. He texted her, obviously. Then he called her, but it went straight to voicemail.

His mind was filled with panicky, unfinished thoughts and unanswered questions. All except the one he should have asked. And all the time he knew he should leave, but to do so would be to accept the unthinkable, the unbearable...

After the first hour the bar staff kept their distance, as if rejection and betrayal were some kind of terrible, contagious disease. By the end of the second hour they were actively avoiding looking at him.

At a little under four hours after he had arranged to meet Dove, he looked up and saw a man strolling into the bar as if he owned it. He had a juddering moment of déjà vu, and then the man was walking towards him, his handsome face lit up with triumph.

'You must be Gabriel Silva.' He stopped next to the table. 'I'm Oscar Cavendish, Dove's father. She's fine,' he added, dropping into the seat opposite. 'There's just been a slight change of plan.' His mouth curled into the smile of a pickpocket palming a wallet. 'I'm afraid she won't be joining you.'

Gabriel stared at him, his brain doing cartwheels. The panic of earlier had returned, and now it was pressing in on him like a thick cloud, sliding over his skin, squeezing his throat.

'I don't understand...' Except he did. He knew exactly what was happening because it had happened before.

'Yes, It's all a bit awkward.' Oscar glanced down at the bag by Gabriel's feet. 'She's had a change of heart.'

Gabriel stared at him, felt his own heart lurching against his ribs. He felt as if Oscar Cavendish had scooped out his stomach and dumped it on the table, and he was grateful that he was sitting down because he felt too hollow to stand.

'She feels dreadful...truly dreadful. She honestly never intended it to get this far. And she hates being the bearer of bad news. Always has. That's why I'm here.'

There was a scraping sound as Gabriel pushed back his chair. 'I want to talk to her. I *need* to talk to her.'

The ache in his voice, the intensity of it, made him flinch. He had never felt more exposed…more powerless. More unwanted.

'I know… I know,' Oscar said soothingly. 'But she doesn't want to talk to you, so it would probably be best for everyone if you just stuck to the plan.' He touched Gabriel's bag with the toe of his hand-made shoe. 'Look, I know it's upsetting, but you're young. You have your whole life ahead of you. You'll find someone who feels the same way. And in the meantime…'

Reaching into his jacket, he pulled out his phone and slid it across the table.

'Your former boss, Bill, is a great friend of the family. He gave me your bank details.' He tapped the screen. 'Dove wanted you to have a little some-thing by way of compensation, so I took the liberty of transferring some money into your account. With the understanding, of course, that she won't be hear-ing from you again.'

It was like a meteor strike. Everything crashed and burned around him, just as it had before. The hotel bar imploded, the table and the undrunk drinks turned to ash, and inside his chest, his heart shat-tered into a million pieces, devastatingly and irre-vocably broken…

* * *

When he finished speaking the silence in the room was sharp-angled, serrated. Dove was staring at him, her gaze frozen on his face.

'That's not what happened.'

She was shaking her head, her grey eyes pure with shock and denial. Actually, her whole body was shaking. He could see her legs and her arms trembling, as if she was standing in a high storm.

'It's not true. You're lying.'

Her eyes were huge and dark and stunned, as if he had hit her.

'He didn't do that. He didn't say those things. He wouldn't do that.'

He stared at her, his heart pounding. He had dreamed of this moment so often, and in his dreams she'd looked just as crushed and diminished as she did now. In his dreams, he revelled in her misery. But now that it was happening for real he didn't feel satisfaction or triumph. He just felt her shock. Her distress. Her pain. As if it was his.

It rolled through him like a pyroclastic cloud, flattening the memory of that day, swallowing up his need for revenge. And what was there to avenge? She had been telling the truth. She had known nothing about what her father had done that day until now.

'I'm sorry, but I'm not lying. Everything I've told you is the truth.'

Not the whole truth—but there was no time or place in the world for that.

She was still staring at him as if he was a stranger. A dark, menacing stranger with a terrible weapon. And he knew only too well that there was no more terrible weapon than a truth you didn't want to hear.

'You didn't send your father.'

It was a statement of fact, but she shook her head as if he had asked a question. 'I was on my way out of the house…on my way to you—' she swallowed, cleared her throat '—and he was waiting for me. I remember being shocked that he was there, scared that he'd found out about us…' Her voice shook around the word. 'And that he was going to stop me. But he just told me that he had something to show me on his phone.'

She was looking past him now, at the stupidly cheerful sun outside the window.

'I didn't understand what I was looking at, at first, and then I did.' Her face seemed to lose shape, like a flower in the wind. 'He told me that he didn't trust you, so he'd gone to find you and offered you money to leave me. And it was there, in black and white, the transfer to your account.' She shivered. 'I never told him to give you money.'

'I know that now.'

He heard her swallow. 'Why did you take it? Why didn't you call me?'

The air was so still the room felt like a tomb. His heart was a dark thud inside his chest.

'I didn't know about the money. He got the account details from Bill. And I don't know why I didn't call you. I suppose I didn't feel there was any-thing to say.'

He had been in shock. After Oscar Cavendish had slithered out of the bar, he'd been shaking so hard it had been another twenty minutes before he could get to his feet.

'Nothing to say?' Her voice had an undertow of misery that made his nails cut into his hands. 'How could you think I would do something like that?'

Easily, he thought. His self-doubt, his fear of rejection…

They'd been like a trail of breadcrumbs, weav-ing through their relationship, so that the whole time they were together a part of him had been waiting for it to happen…hoping it wouldn't, but fearing it would. That at some point Dove would see whatever was in him that had kept his biological mother from wanting him and loving him.

It had just happened sooner than he'd thought it would.

And it had hurt a whole lot more than he could have imagined.

'I didn't think I had any reason to doubt him. I mean, he was your father…'

She flinched, and it tore at him again that she should feel this confusion about her father.

He cleared his throat. 'I was hurt, and angry. I thought you didn't care and I wanted to show you that I didn't care either.'

It was the truth, but not the whole truth.

'I did care—'

Her voice cracked and he reached out for her, but she stumbled backwards, holding her hands in front of her.

'Just leave me alone!' Tears were slipping down her face.

'I can't leave you like this.' He didn't want to leave her.

She tried to push him away, but he wouldn't budge, and finally she leaned into him and he gathered her against his pounding heart.

'It's okay Shh…it's okay.' He sank down on the edge of the bed, pulling her with him. 'It's okay,' he said again, his hand moving in slow, rhythmic circles until finally her sobs subsided.

'I'm sorry,' she whispered. 'I should have called you… I should have known—'

He slid his hands into her hair and tilted her face to his. 'We both made mistakes.'

He felt a sharp stab of guilt. But only he could have put it right at the time. Obviously Dove was going to believe Oscar. He was her *father*. But he could have—*should* have—questioned Oscar's version. He should have confronted Dove. Demanded an explanation. Had he been a different man…a braver man…he would have done so. Instead, he'd let an old truth swamp love and logic. He'd taken the money and walked away, just as he had done a year earlier.

The hardest choice had also been the easiest.

She shifted against him, her hand pushing into

the hard wall of his chest to steady herself, her face lowered. 'It's okay. You can leave. You don't need to stay with me.'

'Is that what you want?' His voice sounded different. Not his own. He knew that he was revealing too much, but he couldn't seem to do anything about it. 'You want me to leave?' he said, over the dark, panicky thud of his heart.

There was a long silence.

He stared down at the top of her head, feeling emotions he couldn't name much less control expanding in all directions.

Moments earlier he had been staggering through the past, dazed and bloodied, hurting and angry. Alone. But somehow they had found their way back to each other, and now the past felt like another world, a distant moon, or a planet far, far away. All that mattered was here and now and the woman in his arms.

As Dove lifted her face to his he could see her pulse beating a wild allegretto against the fragile skin of her throat and he held his breath, knowing that she was feeling it too. And then she was shaking her head, and her soft, 'No…' was lost as he pressed his mouth against hers and kissed her, and everything melted, and there was just his body reaching out to hers…

CHAPTER SEVEN

GABRIEL TOOK A quick breath like a gasp, his fingers reaching to capture her face. She tasted like melted honey, and for a moment he savoured her softness and her sweetness. His hand tightened in her hair and he pulled her closer, pressing against her soft, pliant body, breathing in the scent of sweet-peas and warm skin.

Everything was white and gold and grey, and somewhere over his shoulder he could hear the sea's endless murmur. She moved closer, reaching up to stroke his face, and he felt her fingertips grazing against the stubble on his jaw, light as butterfly wings, then moving lower to his shoulders. And all the time she was kissing him, angling her mouth against his, her teeth catching his lower lip, nipping, teasing...

His heart running wild, maddened by her touch, wanting more, needing more, he broke the kiss and tipped her onto the bed. Stepping back, he yanked his shirt over his head and tossed it on the floor.

His heart was beating inside his head, in time to the thick, urgent pulse of his blood, and he tried to think of the last time he'd felt so out of control.

But then she pulled off her top and wriggled out of her shorts and it was impossible to think. He edged back slightly, the better to admire her small, high breasts in a white cotton bra and the dip of her waist, his body hardening.

She saw it, and her hands reached for him, pressing flat against the outline of his erection, feeling the length and shape of him. He sucked in a breath as a jolt of hunger, hot and sharp like electricity, snaked across his skin, his body stiffening to stone as she unzipped his trousers and freed him.

For a moment he couldn't breathe. His whole body was shivering, as if he was cold, but his skin was on fire. Her fingers curled around the length of him, and then he breathed out jerkily as she leaned forward and he felt the tip of her tongue flick over the blunt head of his erection.

'Ah—' Groaning, he threaded his fingers through her hair, pulling it free so that it spilled over her shoulders like a pale waterfall. She was moving now, dipping lower, licking the shaft, holding him in her mouth...

He swore softly. 'My turn.'

Teeth clenched, he pulled free and nudged her back onto the bed. Breathing unsteadily, he hooked his fingers into her panties and slid them off her body. Her eyes were fixed on his face, narrowed and storm-dark with passion. Leaning forward, he kissed her softly, his thumb shaping her waist and her stomach, moving lower to trace a path through the triangle of white-gold curls.

She rocked towards him, whimpering against his lips, and he slipped his fingers deep inside her, moving them back and forth, feeling her pulse in his hand. Breaking the kiss, he gently parted her legs and crouched over her, breathing in her scent. Her legs were trembling slightly and, sliding his hands under the curve of her bottom, he steadied her, And then he lowered his mouth to the slick heat between her thighs.

Dove arched against his mouth, her fingers digging into his shoulders. Her body was humming like a train track. She could feel the flat of his tongue against the hard nub of her clitoris, feel the muscles inside her clenching as she moved beneath him. The humming inside her was getting louder and louder. She felt soft and ripe and open. Could feel her body coming adrift...

Her fingers flexed against his shoulders. 'I want you inside me...'

He stared at her, his face blunt with the effort of stopping. 'I'll have to go to my room—' he said hoarsely.

'No.' She grabbed his wrist. 'It's fine.'

She pulled him back onto the bed, and his eyes narrowed with a hunger that made her shudder all the way through. He slid her under him, moving against her, his weight on his elbow as he reached down to stroke the head of his erection between her thighs.

Her hands moved to his hips as she felt him push up and she lifted her own hips, felt him push again. And then he was inside her, warm and sleek and hard. He started to move slowly, lifting and lowering like the cresting waves outside, and each time she felt a whisper of liquid heat ripple through her body like a current beneath the water.

It was delicious, and the bliss of it dazzled her.

Her eyelashes fluttered shut and she moaned softly, her hands curving round his arching back, gripping his vertebrae as if she was holding on to the side of a mountain. He was thrusting deeper now, and harder, then deeper still, and she could feel the heat building inside her, fierce, white-hot, stinging.

Her muscles were tightening now, tensing around him, holding him but not holding him. Flames were dancing inside her eyelids. She was burning, melting, chasing the heat, wanting to escape it, yet wanting to make it go on and on and on, wanting it to last for ever, knowing she would die of pleasure if it did—

She shuddered helplessly, her body spasming, tightening and loosening all at once. His mouth found hers and he groaned her name, his muscles snapping tight as he thrust inside her.

Breathing raggedly, Dove gripped his shoulders to steady herself. Her whole body was trembling like a sapling in a storm. She was aware of everything and conscious of nothing. The clean white walls and the shell-pink curtains fluttering in the breeze. The endless blue outside like a Hockney swimming pool. And beside her, inside her, Gabriel, his shuddering breath hot against her throat, his damp skin sticking to hers, so that it was impossible to tell where she ended and he began.

She felt him shift, move his weight, but she couldn't move. She just lay there, trying to breathe. It took a while, and even then it was all her throbbing body and hammering heart would allow her to do for a long time. She knew that there was only him, and there would only ever be him. And the truth of that scared her, and made her want to hold him close for ever, even though she knew it wasn't possible and that this was the end not a new beginning.

For a few seconds she tried to hold herself apart from him, but then she pressed her face against his shoulder, tears spilling onto her cheeks.

'Don't cry.' He kissed the tears off her face, kissed her eyelids, her forehead, her mouth, with gentle, tender kisses that wrenched at her heart. 'I don't ever want to make you cry.'

'It's not you—'

Obviously that wasn't true. Being here with Gabriel's body inside hers was like standing in a thunderstorm on a hill. Like breathing in raw ozone with electricity crackling through her blood. But with it there was the sadness of a summer lost, of days of sunlight and newly cut grass turned to ash in confusion and doubt and a lack of faith.

And then there was the pain of her father's betrayal. Her throat tightened. Betrayal was surely too strong a word. But why, then, did it feel as if the world had broken apart beneath her feet?

She had no idea what could have motivated Oscar to act like that, or why he had said all that stuff about her having a change of heart. For so long she had believed that he had been trying to protect her. Or perhaps more accurately she had *wanted* to believe that he'd been trying to protect her. But the truth was her relationship with her father had been difficult for as long as she could remember. Sometimes he'd been sweet, but often he'd been cold and distant and impossible to like. And then he'd be funny and charming and she'd forget. It was almost as if he hadn't been able to decide how he felt about her.

Gabriel's arm felt warm and heavy against her body. It made her feel safe, secure in a way she hadn't felt in the longest time. Only she knew that she didn't deserve to feel that way.

Her lungs felt as if they might burst. 'I just wish I could go back in time and do things differently,' she whispered. 'If I'd left earlier... I should have left earlier... I should have—'

'Shh...' He pressed his finger against her lips. 'Don't think about that now.'

Gazing up into his eyes was like diving into cool blue water. It soothed the ache in her throat. Curling her arms around his neck, she let him roll her under-neath his body, losing herself in the heat of his kiss. Because even though she knew it wasn't true, it felt as if she was meant for him.

Gazing down at the sleeping woman in his arms, Gabriel felt a jagged weight in his chest. Outside the window the sun was sliding jerkily between clouds, disappearing and then returning to view in time with the beat of his heart.

He had thought he couldn't feel worse than he had that day at the hotel—but then he hadn't truly un-derstood what it felt like to feel someone else's pain.

To be responsible for that pain.

And he *was* responsible. He had let his grief and anger and misery at what had happened with Fenella colour his relationship with Dove. It had been like a bruise, a weakness, and the moment Oscar Cav-endish had pressed against it, it had cracked apart. Blind with panic and pain, he hadn't seen the truth.

Actually, he hadn't looked. It had been easier to accept what he was told, even though doing so meant thinking the worst of the woman he had loved.

He shifted his body, but the guilt was solid... immovable. And he deserved it. If Dove had been a business he was buying he would never have made any decision without completing due diligence. Every single piece of data would have been sifted and analysed and assessed. And yet he had accepted Oscar's words at face value.

Worse, he had acted on what he'd been told without even the most cursory of conversations. Forcing her to work for him, threatening her—threatening her boss, her colleagues—dragging her on to his yacht to rub her face in his wealth and success.

No wonder she had fought him so hard when he'd confronted her at Cavendish and Cox. She must have been devastated by what happened between them. But he had seen it as just temper—frustration at finally being held to account. He had ignored her distress and blackmailed her into working for him anyway.

And he could never make it up to her.

He couldn't change the past—and he certainly couldn't change himself.

His stomach clenched tight. He was broken in some fundamental way. There was a blankness, a gap inside him—like a missing step in a staircase.

He gazed down at Dove. And yet when her body fused with his he felt complete. In those hectic moments he forgot everything…cared about nothing but the light, delicate touch of her fingers and the hot press of her mouth.

Hunger had stormed through him like a conquering army. His hunger and hers. She'd been like a curling flame in his arms. Everything between them had pulled taut, the white heat of their bodies consuming the pain, and the past, so that there had been nothing but fire and need and the bliss of her being his once again.

* * *

Dove stared up at the waterfall, blinking into the cool spray. She had come across it by accident. It had just appeared out of the lush greenery as she'd made her way from the house.

Waking in Gabriel's arms, she had wanted more than anything to stay pressed against his warm, sleeping body. But she knew there was no purpose to thinking like that.

What had happened had not been a mistake. Nothing that perfect could ever be called that. But it would be an act of reckless self-harm to let it happen again. And she didn't trust herself to be there when he woke up. Didn't trust herself to resist that beautiful golden body...

'There you are.'

She turned, her feet slipping on the wet rocks, and steadied herself. Or rather she regained her balance. Nothing could possibly steady her heartbeat, she thought, gazing up into Gabriel's glittering blue eyes.

'I just thought I'd take a quick look around before I left,' she said quickly, trying to pull her mind back in line.

There was a small pause, and then he nodded. 'Of course. But it would probably be better to have a guide. There are quite a few treacherous paths, and it's easy to get lost and not know where you are.'

She frowned. 'Isn't that what being lost is?'

One corner of his mouth twisted into a smile that

kicked up sparks in her all over again, and she was instantly, hopelessly aware of the shimmering blue heat in his eyes and of how close he was standing.

'What I am trying and failing to say is that there's no point using a landmark as a guide if you don't know how it relates to anything else.'

'I see what you mean, yes…' She nodded, but honestly he might have been speaking Portuguese or Mandarin. Her brain didn't seem to be working properly.

'We could walk up to the lake. Or we could head down to the beach. See if we can spot any dolphins.'

'Dolphins?'

He nodded. 'Dolphins, whales, sharks…'

They did see dolphins.

Crouching on an outcrop of rock, Gabriel suddenly pointed out to sea. 'Just there…watch the waves,' he said softly.

Seconds later she saw them. A school of dolphins, ten or twelve maybe, rising and diving in perfect synchronicity, their sleek grey bodies shining in the sunlight as they carved a path through the water with enviable grace.

'Where have they gone?'

Holding up her hand to shield her eyes, Dove squinted into the sunlight, but the dolphins had disappeared from sight, swallowed up by the cresting blue waves.

Gabriel moved beside her. 'Just wait a moment. They'll be back.'

She could feel the vibration of his voice against her shoulder and a flicker of heat skated across her skin. Her palms itched to reach out and touch him again.

'There!'

Her heart skipped and she gasped. A perfect half-sized version of the adult dolphins was leaping effervescently through the water.

'That one's probably just been born. They calve around this time of year.'

She tried to say something, but her chest was churning with a wild joy and a throat-clenching sadness that made speaking impossible.

'Dove…'

Gabriel said her name in that soft, dark way of his, and she felt it ripple through her like warm sunlight. She looked into the sun so that he wouldn't see the tears in her eyes.

'Vai ficar tudo bem.'

He'd spoken in Portuguese. She had no idea what he'd said but it didn't matter, because she was lost somewhere between the softness of his voice and the thumping of her heart.

'It's going to be okay,' he translated. His hand closed around her wrists and he turned her to face him. 'I know you said you wanted to go back to London, and if that's what you still want then you can take the jet and leave tonight.'

'But…?' she prompted.

'I thought you might stay for a couple of days.'

His beautiful face, that she'd once loved to kiss from brow to chin and cheek to cheek, was taut, and his blue eyes were fixed on her face.

'I don't want it to end like this. It feels wrong.'

His words touched her skin like warm drops of rain. Could she stay? Should she stay?

She glanced out to the dancing waves. She could no longer see the dolphins, but she knew that even if she never saw them again, she would always be able to see them in her imagination. And in the same way she knew that if she left now she would carry this sense of sadness and unfinished business with her for ever.

But their relationship wasn't the only unfinished business. 'What about the acquisition?'

She felt his hands tighten around wrists. 'It can wait.' He pulled her closer. 'Carrie can handle things for a couple of days.'

Gazing up into his face, she felt her mouth dry. His gaze was even more blue than usual, and it made her feel as if she was drowning.

Her heart was beating out of time. Would she be mad to stay? Her mother would certainly think so if she knew, but she had no intention of telling her.

What would she say? *Oh, hi, Mum. Just to let you know I'm going to spend a few days having sex with an ex I never mentioned before because Dad paid him to leave me alone and he took the money and broke my heart.*

Okay, some of that was not true anymore, but she

didn't need to ask her mum if this was a good idea. She knew that danger signs should be flashing red inside her head. Wanting him as she did made her vulnerable, but maybe this was the way to break the spell.

Unbidden, a memory swelled up inside her, hot and bright and as clear as if it was happening now. His fingers tangling in her hair, rough and tender, slow and urgent, tracing the line of her mouth...

And his mouth...

She swallowed, heat flooding her body so that her skin was flushed with it. Her breasts were hot and heavy, the nipples pulling tight, and there was a pulse between her thighs. She wanted to kiss his beautiful curving mouth until neither of them could think or breathe. She wanted to tear off his clothes right here and now and lick every inch of his skin. She wanted to pull him inside her and feel him swell and harden, feel him take over her body...

'Okay, then,' she heard herself say. 'I'll stay for a couple of days.'

The next few days were a merry-go-round blur. A head-spinning fever dream of a hunger as deep and endless as the ocean.

It wasn't real. They both knew that.

Maybe that was why it was easy between them— easier than it had been six years ago, when there'd been so many layers of the truth. Now there was just the two of them, in the moment. There was no future, no commitment, no expectation. They lived each minute, each hour.

They ate and drank…walked and swam and slept. And all the time they were touching, stroking, caressing, kissing…revelling in the blissful freedom of being able to slide their hands and mouths over each other's bodies.

And she loved the island. Although it felt like several different islands throughout the day. She loved the smell of the wild mint that grew everywhere. And the way the mountains slid in and out of view between the clouds. She loved the ferns and the moss and the banks of pastel-coloured hydrangeas. Most of all she loved the sea.

Every direction she looked she could see blue— every shade from ink to glass. But there was no blue even in nature that was as beautiful as Gabriel's eyes. And it wasn't just his eyes that set her senses alight.

She glanced up at his face, trying to take everything in—each feature, every tiny shift of expression— wanting to remember. It was what she did every time she looked at him, and she rarely looked away. But still she feared that she would forget something, and the thought almost stopped her heart.

'What are you thinking?' he asked.

He was playing with her hair, running it through his hands, twisting it around his fingers and then unfurling it. Unravelling it.

Unravelling her more, she thought, heat blossoming deep inside her.

'Nothing, really,' she lied.

They were in bed. It was two o'clock in the afternoon. The sun was spilling across his naked body and he was so smooth and golden and gloriously male that it hurt to look at him.

'What are *you* thinking about?' she countered as he drew her head back with a tug of his hand, lowering his mouth to the long line of her throat.

'Me? I was just admiring the view,' he said softly, and she felt the softness in his voice gather low in her belly.

His other hand slid over her stomach to caress the curve of her hip and bottom, his light, precise touch sending little ripples of pleasure across her skin. He lifted his head a fraction and, pulse stumbling, she stared at him, wordless and undone, held captive by the mesmerising blue glitter of his gaze, fascinated by the casual intimacy of his touch, as if all of this was just foreplay. And in a way it was…because there would always be another time.

Until there wasn't.

But she didn't dare think about that. She couldn't think about the moment when she would have to wake from this dream and return to London.

'I thought maybe we could go and look at the vineyard later,' she said quickly.

Things were getting out of hand. She needed to keep some control.

'Today?' His gaze held hers, steady and unblinking. 'It's a bit late. Why don't we go tomorrow?'

'You said that yesterday.'

'And I'll probably say it again tomorrow.'

His gaze moved over her and he smiled then—one of those hesitant almost-smiles that seemed to flip a switch inside her.

'And the day after that...and the day after that...'

She let him pull her closer. She wanted to be closer. Wanted him inside her again...and again and again—

A beat of need pulsed lightly across her skin. Lying here with him, she could feel her feelings growing reckless.

As if he could read her mind, he said softly, 'We could just stay here.'

'We could,' she agreed.

Her pulse jerked as his fingers tiptoed with excruciating slowness down her belly, coming to a stop at the mound of pale curls. She could see his hunger imprinted on his face, the same hunger that was stamped all the way through her, and she was just trying to arrange her face so that he might not realise just how badly she needed him when his phone rang.

He frowned, then hesitated, dragging his eyes away slowly, and with regret. She watched him reach over and pick up the phone.

Glancing at the screen, his frown tugged at his mouth. 'It's Carrie.'

'Answer it,' she said quickly.

His COO would be uber-keen to prove herself capable of steering the ship in Gabriel's absence, so it must be something important for her to get in touch. As he swiped the screen she slipped away to the bathroom to give him some privacy, grateful for the breathing space.

It was dangerous to let herself think about for ever. Even if her own failed attempt at a relationship could be excused, she had watched her parents' marriage limp on until death had parted them. But they were not unique, and she needed to remember that the next time she started telling herself stories which ended with happy-ever-after.

This was sex—and that was all it could ever be, she told herself as she walked back into the bedroom.

Gabriel was facing the window, but she didn't need to see his face to know that something was wrong. The phone was wedged against his ear, and even though he was no longer naked there was a visible tension in his shoulders.

'It's not up to her. If she's got a problem with it, she needs to talk to her s-son—' As he stumbled over the word, he turned and saw her hovering in the doorway.

'I need to go. Keep me updated.' He rang off and tossed the phone onto the bedside table.

'Is there a problem?' she asked quietly.

Reaching for her bathrobe, she slipped her arms into the sleeves and knotted it around her waist.

'You could say that.' The skin on his face was pulled taut and his voice was stretched even tighter. 'Fenella Ogilvy is kicking off about the name-change.'

Dove stared at him in silence. Name-changes were not unusual in acquisitions. The interim chairman of the company, Fenella Ogilvy's son, Angus, had already agreed to lose the name, but clearly he hadn't squared things with his mother.

'What does she want?'

'It doesn't matter—it's not happening.'

She frowned. 'What's not happening?'

'She wants to meet with me.' His words were clipped and cold. The ease and intimacy between them earlier had evaporated as quickly as the mist around the mountain.

'Okay...' she said slowly. 'It's a family firm. Sometimes shareholders, particularly family members get jumpy about their legacy. You know that. Maybe if she met you—'

'I'm not meeting her. I'm not ready.'

Not ready?

She stood in the doorway, staring at him uncertainly. That was just not true. Gabriel was easily the most capable, most informed person on the team. 'I don't understand what you mean by "ready"...' she said slowly.

'You don't need to understand.' His eyes were as hard and flat as his voice. 'You're just a cog in a wheel, remember?'

She flinched—more than she'd meant to. But his harshness was like a blow to the head. Before when he said those same words they had both still been smarting from old betrayals, lashing out, wanting to hurt.

It was supposed to be different now. Together they had worked through the lies and the mistakes of the past to find the truth—their truth. A truth that might not mean they had the same relationship as before, but it wasn't this either. A sniping range where old anger was used like armour-piercing ammunition.

She didn't want this…didn't want to be like Oscar and Olivia…

The thought made her reach out and brace her hand against the doorframe. The old Dove—the Dove who had soothed and conciliated such outbursts—would have counselled calm, but she wasn't the old Dove anymore and, lifting her chin, she said coolly, 'Please don't talk to me like that. It's rude and unnecessary.'

His eyes snapped to her face, the blue choppy with anger and frustration and an emotion she didn't recognise.

'Blunt, not rude. But I agree it was unnecessary. I shouldn't need to remind you that some decisions are above your paygrade.'

Her heart was pounding, but she kept her gaze, deliberate and unflinching. 'I know that. But that still doesn't give you the right to speak to me in that way.'

His eyes locked with hers, his face taut and pale against the shadow of his stubble. 'Why? Because we're having sex?'

'Actually, yes.' Now she was angry. 'I don't just

sleep with anyone, Gabriel.' *Make that nobody in the last six years.* 'I'm sleeping with you because I like you and I care about you, even when we're not having sex. I thought you felt the same way. Clearly I was wrong.'

'Clearly.'

There was a brittle, crushing silence.

She stared at him, hurt, angry, disbelieving, her mind jolting against the shock of his words. 'Why are you being like this? What is wrong with you?'

He spun away and walked towards the window. She stared after him, still angry, but something in the set of his shoulders made it impossible for her to just walk away. There was an ache in her chest, and she pressed her hand against it. Seconds earlier she had told him she cared, and if that was true then she couldn't walk away. His anger was defensive. She knew that. He was pushing her away to protect himself. Only from what?

She stared at his back, feeling his anger like an uncut diamond scraping over her skin, and at the same time she realised that there was something else—something bigger than his anger. Something like fear, only not fear. It was a gap in him...a hollow that she badly wanted to fill so that he could be whole.

'You are ready, Gabriel.'

He was shocked. Not at her words, which he couldn't hear above the pounding of his heart, but at her not leaving. He had wanted her to leave—needed her to leave. So that he could go back to blaming her, hating her. And she should hate *him*; he was being cold and cruel. But she was still here, and that was intolerable. Or it should be intolerable. Only it wasn't. It was a relief.

'You are ready,' she said again, and now he heard her.

But he wasn't.

Blood roaring in his ears, Gabriel stared out at the huge dark peak. He could have stalked over to the other window, that overlooked the sea, but for some reason he was drawn to the mountain. Maybe because, like him, it was the legacy of something intense and unplanned.

Unlike him, it didn't have to think about what that meant…

The idea of meeting Fenella pressed against a bruise inside him that had never healed.

He could feel Dove's gaze on his back and he wanted to tell her that she was right. He *had* been rude, not blunt, and deliberately so. Because she was there, and he was feeling small enough to need to lash out at someone. Only then he would have to explain why he'd needed to lash out, and that would be a slippery slope.

He had kept so much hidden for so long for a reason.

Keeping his gaze fixed on the mountain, he

shrugged as if his heart was beating normally. 'It's complicated,' he said.

For a moment she didn't respond, and then she took a step towards him, then another 'So simplify it,' she said. 'If you had to sum up the problem with Fenella in three words, what would you say?'

He turned, opening his mouth to tell her another lie, but then he saw her face. Sunlight was illuminating her features and he could see that she was worried. *About him.* And it was the simplicity of that fact that stunned him into speaking, into telling her the truth.

'She's my mother.'

CHAPTER EIGHT

IT WAS THE first time he had said those words out loud, and he half expected the world to fall away beneath his feet and that he would slide into the crack. But Dove's grey eyes steadied him.

'My birth mother,' he added, in case she hadn't understood.

But of course she had.

Only she didn't know everything.

She probably thought he was upset at having been given up for adoption. She didn't know that his mother had turned away from him twice.

'I didn't know you were adopted.'

'It never came up.' *Obviously.*

It had been up to him to share that particular truth, but telling someone when you first met would be weird, and if you didn't say anything then it got harder and harder to think of a way to just drop it into the conversation. And anyway it had felt disloyal to Luis and Laura, who were his parents in every way that it was possible to be a parent.

'When did you find out?' she asked.

'That I was adopted?' He frowned. 'I can't re-member not knowing. I don't remember my par-ents sitting me down and telling me on a particular day. They were just always open about it—but in a good way. They made it seem that their adopting me wasn't about solving some horrible mess. It was a way for us to build a family. I think that's why I didn't actually even think about my birth parents for a very long time.'

If only he had kept on feeling that way, then maybe he would never have hurt this beautiful, clear-eyed woman. She could have stayed safe and happy in her beautiful clean world, far away from the mess and turmoil in his head.

'What changed?'

The steadiness in her voice pulled him back, and he felt some of the turmoil ease. He felt again the shock of her being there with him, caring enough to stay there. It was the same shock and gratitude and disbelief that he'd felt the first time she had turned and talked to him.

'We found out that my brother, Tom, was a haemo-philiac. It's carried in the female line, and I suppose it made me think about my mother. My biological mother. And the more I thought, the more questions I had. What was she doing now? Did I look like her? Why did she give me up for adoption?'

And then, later, did she regret giving me up? Would she love me if she was given a second chance?

'Did you ask your parents about her?'

The directness of Dove's questions surprised him. But then again so much about her surprised him.

'No.' He shook his head. 'They would have helped me…supported me…but I felt bad that I wanted to know. Like I was judging them.' His throat felt scratchy. 'And they don't deserve that. They're good people.'

Like you, he thought, glancing over at her, seeing the concern in her grey eyes.

'I didn't do anything about it for a long time, and then, about eighteen months before I met you, I went to an appointment at the hospital with my brother and there was a poster in the waiting room about finding your birth parents. I suppose it felt like fate.'

Her eyes held his. 'So you decided to contact her?'

He nodded. 'It took about six months after I decided to get in touch to do anything about it.

'In the end I sent her a letter. I put my phone number in it.' He paused, remembering how it had felt… the thrill, the fear, the guilt, the hope. 'The agency told me that I needed to be positive, but realistic. Often birth mothers didn't want to be contacted. But she texted me almost immediately, suggesting we meet at a hotel.'

His throat felt so tight it hurt when he swallowed.

'I was nervous, but excited. I bought her flowers. Tulips. I was early, and she was late, but I thought she was probably nervous too.'

He glanced away, staring across the room, seeing again the hotel bar with its scratched dark wood tables and worn armchairs. It had been clean, but shabby, and a long way out of town. He should have known then what she had planned, but he hadn't been thinking straight.

'I was checking my phone when this man walked in. I remember thinking that he was way smarter than everyone else. Wearing a proper suit and polished leather shoes. He seemed to be looking for someone, and I thought he must be having an affair.' He laughed roughly. 'But then he saw me, and he came over and asked if I was James Balfour.'

His pulse jerked as he said the name, and he waited for his heart to steady itself...waited until it was easier to carry on.

'That's the name on my birth certificate,' he said finally.

Dove nodded, which was more than he had managed to do at the time. He'd felt as if he was floating, looking down on himself. Except that he wasn't Gabriel—he was James. A stranger talking to another stranger in an unfamiliar bar.

For weeks afterwards he hadn't been able to look in the mirror in case he saw no reflection. Even the memory of it now was doing something strange to the air, making it hiss like an untuned radio.

'Who was he?'

Dove's voice cut across his thoughts.

'His name was Charles Lambton. He was a lawyer. My mother's lawyer. You see, I'd got it wrong.'

He couldn't keep the shake out of his voice. 'She wasn't late. She wasn't coming. In fact, she hadn't even texted me. Lambton had.'

'What did he say?'

This was one of the reasons he had never told anyone about what happened that day. The questions they would ask that he couldn't answer. But it was different with Dove. Her quiet voice helped. Like a hand on his arm, guiding him through a treacherous landscape.

'Not much. It was very civilised, very polite, but we didn't make small talk. He apologised for "the subterfuge", I think he called it, and told me his client had decided against meeting me in person. She thought it would be better to send a trusted third party.'

He had been stunned, unprepared. Around him, the colour had drained from the bar, so that the tulips on the seat beside him had looked overblown and obvious.

'Better in what way?'

His stomach snapped tight. He felt vulnerable, panicky. This was always the worst part to remember—that and the bit that had followed. Usually whenever he got there he couldn't seem to make the room stay still. The first time it had happened at work he'd had to hold on to the desk to stop it moving. Mostly he had a whisky to get past it. Or he went for a run and kept on running until his lungs screamed and his muscles ached more than his chest and it was as if it had never happened.

Only Dove's questions were like a crack in a dam, and the truth was a swell of water pushing against it. It was impossible to hold it back, but somehow that made it easier for his words to flow.

'She had—*has*,' he corrected himself, 'a life. A husband. A daughter. A s-son. He's three years younger than me.' He heard his own voice, the stammer, clumsy and stupid like a child, and he didn't know what hurt more. That she had gone on to have another family so soon after she'd discarded him or that it hadn't made her think about him.

'Oh—and her family has a property company.' He felt his mouth twist into something like a smile, but not, because smiles shouldn't hurt.

'Basically, the gist of it was that she didn't want everything good in her life ruined because of a drunken one night stand on a Portuguese beach.'

In the past, when he'd thought about shining a light into the dark corners of his life, what had stopped him was the certainty that nobody else would want to look. But now the sun was streaming into the room, turning everything gold, and Dove was still there.

He stared at her, feeling lightheaded.

'I was a mistake. A secret, unwanted mistake. And that's why she gave me up for adoption. So that I would stay a secret. She wasn't looking for a second chance. There was no place for me in her life, and nothing would change.'

It sounded ugly. It *was* ugly. But Dove didn't flinch or look away, as if he too was ugly. Instead, she reached out and took his hand.

He stared down at her soft fingers, feeling not just their softness but their strength, and he took that strength and said, 'Then Charles Lambton took out an envelope and pushed it across the table. He told me that his cilent wanted to give me something to compensate for any distress I might have felt.'

Dove stared at him in silence. Her throat was so tight she could hardly breathe. 'Oh, Gabriel…'

'I thought it would be different. I mean, I can see why having a baby on your own when you were nineteen would be difficult, but she didn't even want to meet me—'

The skin on his face was stretched taut across the bones, and without thinking she stepped forward and slid her arms around him. 'I'm so sorry,' she whispered.

No wonder he had been so devastated when her father had walked into that hotel bar. No wonder he had taken the money and left. It would have felt like *déjà vu*—or rather *déjà vecu*. And now she knew why he hadn't told her any of this before. She knew because telling people things that were hard to hear, to know, to accept, was almost impossible.

She knew because she had spent her life *not* telling people those things.

But he had done it.

Her arms tightened around his body and it was then, holding his body tightly, feeling Gabriel's heart beating against hers, or maybe her heart beating against his, that Dove understood that she loved him. He was in her heart and he had never not been—no matter how much she had tried to forget about him.

For a moment she couldn't do anything but lean into him. She was shaking inside with shock. And yet a part of her had always known. That was why she hadn't called his bluff back in London. And why, before that, she had found it so easy to stay single. For her, there had never been any other man but Gabriel. She just couldn't imagine anyone but him kissing her, touching her, holding her.

Her pulse shivered and her hands trembled against his shoulders. The urge to tell him the truth was overwhelming. But there were other truths in the tense way he held his body.

She looked up into his face, seeing the boy beneath the man. Right from the start she had questioned why he wanted Fairlight Holdings so badly. The business had some plus points, but there were far better investments. None, though, as owned by the family of his birth mother, and that was the reason he was doing all this. To prove himself to Fenella Ogilvy and perhaps finally forge a connection with her.

'That's what this is about, isn't it?' she said softly. 'You want to give her another chance.'

'Another chance?'

He was staring at her, his blue eyes narrow on her face as he stepped back out of her embrace. His mood had changed. The anger was back.

'I don't want to give her another *chance*. I don't want anything to do with her. When the acquisition is signed off, and her family's business is mine, then I'll send someone to meet her in a hotel of my choosing—just to let her know that everything her family once owned now belongs to *me*. The son she gave up. The son who wasn't good enough.'

Dove held her breath. She had been wrong. The anger had never left him. It was always there...like his shadow. Her stomach knotted and her heart was beating very hard. She knew first-hand the consequences of living with anger and resentment day in and day out. It was corrosive and crushing. Even her father, who had seemed outwardly to thrive on it, had not been a happy man.

The thought of Gabriel turning into her father made her stomach cave in on itself.

'And then what?' she said quietly.

He frowned, his anger still there. 'I walk away and get on with my life.'

Dove stared at him, feeling his words chafing beneath her skin, seeing her own life. The arguments... her father's inexplicable cold anger. Her mother's equally inexplicable refusal to leave, trapped, fused with her father in some baffling mix of money and manners and fear and loathing and helplessness.

She shook her head. 'Walking away isn't closure, Gabriel. We both know that. Because if it was you and I wouldn't be here now, having this conversation.'

'That's different.'

'Is it?'

She bit her lip, hating the tension in his face. The coiled-up pain of his birth mother's rejection was visible in the taut set of his shoulders and the bunching of muscles beneath his shirt. He could barely hold it in. But the acquisition would only be a temporary fix. A Band-Aid, she thought, her stomach knotting around the word.

But a sticking plaster was only for cuts and grazes. It couldn't fix a mother's rejection. Or a doomed marriage.

'I know you're angry, and hurt, and you have every right to be. Your mother was wrong to do what she did—but it was seven years ago. Things are different now. *You're* different now. Maybe if you talk to her…say what you want to say—'

'I tried that once before, remember?'

There was no softness to his beautiful face. He looked like an angel carved of stone…stern, unforgiving, locked in with his anger and misery for eternity.

'And what? You can't try again? Give her a second chance?'

'I don't do second chances.' There was a hard edge to his voice.

She lifted her chin. 'You gave me one.'

'That's different,' he said again.

'But it isn't.'

Her heart was pounding fast, as if she was running, and she wished that she was. But there was nowhere left to run from the truth. His or hers.

'I know it's hard to let go, but believe me—whatever punishment you think you're meting out to Fenella Ogilvy won't be enough,' she said flatly. 'It wasn't enough for my parents. You'll just end up punishing yourself.'

Her ribs tightened as his blazing blue eyes lifted to hers.

'I thought your parents loved one another,' he said.

She felt suddenly fragile. That was what she had told him all those years ago, out of necessity and fear and shame. But after everything he had told her she couldn't pretend any longer.

'I lied to you. I didn't mean to. I thought I could tell you the truth. But then you showed me that photo of your family at Christmas. You all looked so happy, and your dad was looking at your mum as if they were unconquerable—'

Her throat felt hot and heavy, and she knew that it was full of all the tears she had never cried. For him. For her parents. For herself.

'Nobody I've ever known feels like that—certainly not my parents. Maybe they were in love right at the beginning, but then I think my mother realised that what my father really loved was her inheritance. When she found that out she punished him by keeping him short of money. So he punished her by having countless affairs with her friends.'

Gabriel was staring at her, his beautiful face blank of expression, but she knew how it sounded.

'Where did you fit in?' he asked.

'Me?'

She knew her mouth had moved to curve into a smile, but her voice sounded raw and tight, as if it hurt to speak.

'I was the Band-Aid baby. One last attempt to make things work. And it did for a bit. And then it didn't.'

Her lips were aching now.

'Sometimes they would be okay for a day or two, and then my dad would goad my mum and it would all kick off. My mother would go so far, but Oscar would always go further. *Too* far. And I knew it was my fault. I knew they were only together because of me. So I'd try to head things off. That was my job. To find ways to defuse the tension and smooth things over.'

'Problem-solving...' he said slowly.

Remembering the conversation they'd had on *The Argentum*, about why she had chosen corporate law, she nodded. It was why she lived her life as she had, coolly distant from intimacy and any kind of dependency.

Until Gabriel.

And then she had wanted him so badly, and in wanting him she'd forgotten that she knew nothing of how relationships were meant to work.

'I know I shouldn't have lied, but when you showed me that photo I panicked. I was scared that if I told you the truth—if I told you that my parents had spent their marriage hating one another—you might see things differently. See *us* differently. So you're right. I did lie to you. I lied because you made me want the thing that scared me most of all.'

Love, and the possibility of love everlasting.

Lying in his bed, with his arms wrapped around her and sunlight and birdsong filling the room, for the first time she'd had love and hope and faith. And it had been intoxicating—*he* had been intoxicating. But she should have known then how it would end. With lies and confusion and regrets.

She looked away before he could see her tears. Before she could see his face change. She didn't want to go back to the way he had looked at her in London, with so much anger and contempt. So much distance.

'What was it that you wanted?'

He spoke so quietly that at first she thought she had imagined his voice. But then he said it again.

'What was it that you wanted?'

She wanted it still. More than she ever had. Because now she knew him. But she couldn't tell him that. There was too much history. Too much hurt.

'I wanted you. I wanted us. Before, I'd thought

a relationship…marriage…was just a trap, a cage. But you made it feel like danger and freedom and safety all at once.'

It was only as he reached out and pulled her closer that she realised she had spoken the words out loud. She felt naked and young and stupid, and terrified that he would see too much—see the love she still felt for him. She buried her face against his shoulder.

'I felt the same way.'

His cheek was warm against her, and his body was strong and so, so comforting, but still she couldn't look at him.

'Dove—'

She felt him slide his hands into her hair, and then he tilted her face up to him, forcing her to look at him.

'I'm sorry. For making you work for me. For threatening you. Threatening Alistair. I shouldn't have done it. I knew it was wrong, but I was angry. With you. With myself. With everything and everyone.' He dropped his hands and his face twisted. 'I'm always angry. I don't want to be, but it's—'

He broke off and, seeing his pain, feeling his fatigue, she felt her heart crack in two.

'I'm so tired of feeling like this all the time. That's why I have to make this acquisition happen. So I can move on. And I *need* to move on. But I'm not going to force you to stay and do something you're not comfortable with.'

'Are you firing me?' she asked, struggling to keep

her voice steady. To keep looking at him as if there was something more inside her than the terrible silent scream that was breaking her ribs apart.

His hands caught hers. 'No, but if you stay it has to be of your own free will. And if you choose to leave there won't be any repercussions. I don't think I made that clear before.'

There was a perfect stillness.

Did he really think that was why she had stayed?

He was holding her loosely, his thumbs resting against the soft white underside of her wrists. But she felt the press of his thumbs in every part of her body.

Her eyes found his. He was giving her a choice. Only there was no choice. Because she didn't want to leave. She didn't want to lose him. Not yet, anyway.

'I want to stay,' she said quietly.

Stretched between the silence and the drumming of his heart, Gabriel felt his body soften with relief. Only a few days ago he had asked Dove to stay.

'I don't want it to end like this. It feels wrong,' he had said.

And she had stayed.

Only he couldn't bear thinking that it was because of the threats he'd made back in London, and then again on the yacht. Nor could he bear the idea of her leaving, even though he knew that she had every right to go.

And yet, incredibly, she was choosing to stay. Even though he knew that she would never do this—

seek revenge after so long. But he didn't know another way to finish what his birth mother had started.

All he knew was that Dove was here, and that he couldn't stop staring at the hollows of her collarbone and the pulse beating in her throat.

The air quivered around them.

She moved first, reaching up to brush her lips against his, so softly that if his eyes had been shut he would have thought it was nothing but his imagination. But then she leaned in and kissed him on his mouth, and all over his face, licking him, nipping his skin, her breath warm and sweet.

His pulse jolted as she pressed her hand to his trousers, flattening her fingers inside the waistband.

At first there was just the need for her...the need to taste her again and know that she was his. Only that wasn't enough. He wanted more.

Heart pummelling his ribs, he slid his hands under her robe and pulled her towards him. She made a soft, choking noise against his mouth, and the sound snagged all five senses and made his breath chafe in his throat.

Her skin was warm and smooth, like satin, and it seemed to melt under his touch. But still he wanted more.

He tugged the belt around her waist, loosening it so that the robe slipped from her shoulders, and now she was naked. Pulse accelerating, he stared at her, feeling her nakedness and her nearness go through him.

She was exquisite. If she were a drawing it would be nothing more than a few curving lines. His eyes lingered on her nipples, then dropped to her thighs. And some light shading, he thought, his body shuddering into a hardness that made his legs sway beneath him.

They kissed again and then she broke away. But she left her hand inside his trousers, stroking him, smoothing her thumb over the swollen heavy head of his erection, her touch igniting a blaze of need, her soft, hungry grey gaze sliding straight through him, undoing him, making him shake…

Grunting, he batted her hand away, pushing her back on the bed and stripping off his clothes. She lay there watching him, her limbs sprawled against the sun-soaked sheets, her hair spilling over the pillow like rays of sunlight, and all of her seemed to be golden and white.

And then her hand reached for him, and he stopped seeing, stopped thinking, and his mind was nothing but heat and need.

Lost in her beauty, scraped raw and aching with desire, he lowered his mouth to her breast, tasting her there, teasing first one nipple then the other, feeling them swell and harden, feeling her body squirming restlessly against him as her hands splayed against his back, and it was sweet and slow and irresistible…

Dove shivered inside all the way through. She felt as if Gabriel was tuning her body…each touch, each lick, each caress sounding out a different note inside her…and she was lost in the shimmering vibrations breaking over her skin in a lazy, sensual rhythm that lifted her outside herself.

She wanted, wanted, *wanted* him. Only Gabriel could make her feel so whole and yet so prised wide open.

'Do you like that?'

His voice, the hoarseness of it, prised her open a little more, just as if he was using his mouth, his tongue, to part her legs and tease the coiling heat that pulsed there.

'Yes…'

Her breasts felt heavy, the taut peaks of her nipples pulled so taut that it hurt when he touched them. But it hurt more when he didn't. She arched upwards, pushing against his hard, seeking mouth, and then he was rolling over, taking her with him so that she was on top.

'I want to see you. All of you,' he said, in that same hoarse way that made her breath spin out of her throat and her heart beat light and fast like the wings of a hummingbird.

His hands were flush against her hips and he lifted her up, moving her forward, then back, so that the blunt tip of his erection was rubbing her clitoris. It felt so good…made everything inside her swell and curl like a wave.

'Like that,' she whispered. 'Just like that.'

Her head tipped back. She couldn't get enough.

And when he lifted her again she shifted her weight, her hands finding him, guiding him between her legs.

He sucked in a breath, sharply, and she felt his hunger sweep through her like a rolling sheet of flame.

'Yes. *Yes.*'

She tilted her hips to his, pushing down, feeling him fill her, arching her body. His blue eyes were dark with the heat that flooded her limbs. His fingers were pulling at her nipples, pinching them lightly, stroking the taut flesh, and all the time he was moving against her, his hardness filling her, his hands anchoring her against him as he pushed harder, deeper, harder, deeper...

Her nails dug into his arm.

'Let go.' He reached up and pulled her mouth to his, 'Let go,' he said again, and he pulled her closer, then closer still, and she tensed.

A bolt of lightning whipped through her, hot, stinging, making her body twitch and jerk over and over. She gasped, then cried out, and he licked the sounds from her trembling mouth. And then he was tensing, shuddering against her, dragging her hips down and thrusting up inside her, making her splinter and fly apart into a thousand glittering shards.

Breathing unsteadily, she folded against him. For a moment they lay together, panting, spent, and then he lifted her to one side, moving her under his hard, muscular body, stretching out above her.

The maleness of him set her alight. His hand was tight in her hair. His face was serious, his blue eyes blazing with a light that she could feel inside.

'I've never wanted any woman the way I want you—'

She felt his mouth on her throat, as if he needed her pulse to live, and she held him tight, wondering what it would take for that to be true.

Then he lifted his head, shifting his weight so that they were side by side.

'How would you feel about going to New York?' he asked. He stroked her tangled blonde hair away from her face. 'I'm supposed to be going to a dinner there on Friday—some charity event. I was going to cancel and just send in a donation, but why don't you come with me?'

'To New York?'

'Why not? We don't actually have to go to the event. We could just go out on our own,' he said softly. 'Have dinner...see a show.'

She stared at him, mesmerised by the softness in his eyes, terrified by the longing that had sneaked into her heart at his suggestion.

'Does that make me your date?' She gave a mock frown. 'Only I thought I was a distraction.'

'Can't you be both?'

She felt the press of his erection against her stomach, hard where she was soft, and instantly forgot the question.

'I don't know,' she said helplessly.

'But I do—and the answer is yes, you can. So come with me,' he said again. 'If you need an excuse for Alistair we could always drop in at my office. I can show you around. After you've finished distracting me,' he added.

And then he smiled, and she felt it ripple through her, making her yearn for him all over again.

Her hot, damp skin was sticking to his and she could feel his heart beating in time with hers. They were seamless…fused with need.

But it was not just need for her, she thought, and had to press her hand against her mouth to stop herself from declaring her love for him.

What would be the point? For Gabriel, this was sex. She knew he felt the familiarity of it, but he wasn't offering her a future, just dinner and show. And a personal tour of his office. Business and pleasure.

But not love.

'I don't need an excuse,' she said, smiling up at him casually, pretending that she wanted nothing more than to distract, and be distracted by him.

And then Gabriel leaned in and kissed her, and she didn't have to pretend any more.

CHAPTER NINE

GAZING OUT OF the window of his private jet, Gabriel tried to let his thoughts drift in time to the clouds gliding past the glass.

It wasn't easy. The clouds passed by smoothly, like swans on water, but his thoughts were stop-start, jerking back and forth between the past and the present, between Dove and Fenella Ogilvy. He was running from the past, from the mother who had pushed him away not once but twice, and he hated it that he was the kind of man who did that.

But the idea of meeting her just yet was beyond him.

Better to concentrate on the present, and on the woman sitting beside him. The woman who had stayed with him when he'd pushed her away, and then stood by him, literally holding his hand, while he shared the secrets he had held close for so long.

He glanced to where Dove sat opposite him, her grey eyes lowered to the book in her lap. They had talked again, about her father and his mother, and he knew that she was still struggling to understand Oscar Cavendish's actions six years ago. But, unlike him, she wasn't fighting the truth. She had accepted it. Maybe because her father was gone.

No, he thought, his eyes seeking Dove again, as they did roughly every two minutes. She didn't fight. She solved problems. If Oscar had still been alive, she would have been trying to find a way to live with the consequences, not dwelling on what couldn't be changed.

She hadn't tried to get him to talk to Fenella again. Instead, she had suggested that he write a letter.

'You don't have to send it,' she'd said. 'Just write down everything you want to say to her and maybe then, when everything's clear in your head, you could arrange to meet her on your terms.'

He understood the theory, and he'd half listened to her, but there had been a small indentation in her forehead that had kept distracting him. But then there seemed to be no end to the things about Dove which distracted him.

There was her voice.

That sweet smile that seemed to light up her skin and fill him with light too.

The softness of her hair.

And that hollow at the base of her neck. It was exactly the right size for his thumb, and he liked to rest it there, feeling her pulse.

His hand twitched and he wondered what she

would do if he reached over and cupped her head
and held her like that now and for ever—

For ever?

The words hovered in the cool cabin air, dancing
in front of his eyes like light reflecting off water,
and he felt a calmness that was also a kind of eu-
phoria. *For ever with Dove.* Waking with her every
day and taking her into his bed every night and all
the hours in between...

But what was he thinking?

His chest tightened. There was no 'for ever' for
him and Dove. How could there be? She knew him
too well to want anything beyond these few days and
nights they had set aside to say goodbye properly.
That was all he had to offer. And it was the least he
could do to make up for the appalling way he had
treated her.

For all the appalling things in her life.

He stared out of the window, his throat closing
over. Listening to her talk about her parents' marriage, he had felt numb with shame and self-loathing.
All the time they'd been together, and all the years
that had followed, when he had condemned her without trial, right up to the moment when he had bullied
her into working for him, he had been so certain that
he alone had suffered.

But Dove had been hurting all this time. Everything he'd thought he'd known about her was wrong.
She had suffered too.

And then there was the acquisition. Dove was

right. Things were different now. He wasn't a penniless young man any more. He was fully grown, and very wealthy and successful.

His fingers tapped out a rhythm on the armrest. But she was wrong about other things. Outwardly he might have changed, but inside everything had stayed the same. The wound of his mother's rejection was as raw now as it had been seven years ago. And he couldn't do it. He couldn't go and talk to Fenella. He couldn't put himself in the position of being rejected again.

Unlike Dove.

Remembering how she had hidden away on *The Argentum* and confronted him, he stilled his fingers. She was brave in a way he simply couldn't be. That was why things had to be done his way. So that he could leave Fenella Ogilvy and James Balfour behind for ever. It was what he had been working towards for almost a third of his life.

'What is it?'

He glanced up. Dove was staring at him, her grey eyes resting on his face, her expression a mix of confusion and concern.

'Nothing,' he lied. 'I was just thinking about which show we could go to.'

He knew she was worried about him. Knew, too, that she had agreed to stay because of the way he had spoken about his mother. He had seen the shock and fear in her eyes, and it sickened him that he'd scared her.

What he wanted was to take care of her, to protect her. Except that wouldn't work because he wanted to protect her from men like himself and her father. Men who were damaged irretrievably. Men whose anger at the world made them forget the rules.

'We don't have to do a show. I mean, we probably won't be able to get tickets at such short notice.'

'Don't worry about that. In fact, don't worry about anything. Just leave everything to me.'

He leaned forward and cupped the back of her head in his hand, his pulse jerking as he fitted his thumb into the hollow there. They had only been in the air an hour, and they had made love multiple times before they'd left. The last time he had dragged her upstairs to the bedroom, lifting her against the door, both of them panting and fully clothed. But, he wanted her still—always.

Leaning forward, he pulled her towards him, tilting her head up to meet his, fitting his mouth to hers. Her fingers fluttered against his arms and he knew that she wanted what he wanted.

They made it to the cabin, mouths fusing, hands pulling at each other as they fell onto the bed.

Somewhere nearby a phone started ringing. Not his, but he could feel Dove tensing. Groaning, he reached over and picked up the phone, frowning down at the screen. 'It's your mother.'

She hesitated. 'It's probably nothing. She just likes to catch up. I'll call her back.'

Her mouth found his as the ringing stopped and he pulled her closer, his fingers loosening around the phone as everything else tightened.

He swore under his breath as the ringing started again. But, catching sight of Dove's face, he tamped down his hunger.

'It's fine.' Shifting away from the soft, seductive warmth of her body, he handed her the phone. 'But just so you know…we have four hours of flight time left and I intend to spend every remaining minute of those hours in this bed with you.'

'Hi, Mum.' She kissed him lightly on the lips. *I won't be long*, she mouthed.

Given his current state of arousal, any amount of time was too long, he thought, rolling back against the pillow, his heartbeat slowing to match the pulse in his groin. He felt a burst of heat as she leaned forward and he caught a glimpse of the back of her neck. Four hours in bed wasn't going to be enough to satisfy his need for this woman. That would take several lifetimes. In fact, he would probably need until the end of time itself.

'But what did they say? Is he going to be all right?'

The breathless shock in Dove's voice cut across his musings like a guillotine. His eyes snapped over to where she was sitting, her hand clenched around the phone, the knuckles stark against her pale skin.

'What is it?' He was by her side in an instant. 'What's happened?' he asked gently.

'It's Alistair. He's been taken into hospital.' She pressed her hand against her mouth. 'My mum couldn't get him to wake up, and when she did his speech was all slurred.'

Dove was struggling to speak, and there were tears in her eyes.

'He must have had a stroke. Or maybe it's his diabetes.'

Her voice was muffled by her knuckles but still he could hear her pain.

'My dad died before I got to the hospital—'

'That won't happen.' The pain in her voice made him want to tear the plane apart with his bare hands. 'I won't let that happen.'

Staring down into her pale, desperate face, he felt his heart swell. Nothing mattered except making her happy and whole again. Not the acquisition. Not his own pain. There was only Dove.

He knew in that moment that he loved her, and the urgency of it filled his mouth—only this wasn't the right time. Dove needed him to step up. She needed someone she could rely on.

'It's okay.' He pulled her against him. 'Listen to me. It's going to be okay.'

He took the phone from her hand, deliberately slowing his mind, blanking out his love for her and her heart-wrenching panic.

'Mrs Cavendish? It's Gabriel Silva. I'm here with your daughter. Could you tell me which hospital Alistair was taken to?'

* * *

For Dove, the next three hours were a nightmarish blend of time moving with agonising slowness and holding her breath, waiting for the phone to ring again.

She felt another wave of panic rise up inside her. Everything was jerky and disconnected. Her breath, her thoughts. And she couldn't stop the tears from rolling down her face.

If she had been on her own, she had no idea how she would have got back to London. But she wasn't on her own. Gabriel was with her.

After hanging up the phone, he'd taken charge immediately. Within minutes the plane had turned round and headed towards London. Next, he'd called ahead to arrange for a driver to meet them at the airport, and all the time he'd been making calls and organising people he'd been by her side, the quiet, solid strength of his body giving her strength.

And now they were heading towards the hospital in a limousine, and she was having to tense every muscle to stop herself crying out when the car stopped at a red traffic light.

'He's in good hands.'

She turned to where Gabriel sat beside her. His blue eyes were steady and calm on her face and she let out a long, slow breath. He sounded so sure, so certain.

'I just wish I knew what was going on.'

'You will. We're less than five minutes away from

the hospital now. But in the meantime just try and focus on what you do know—which is that your mother acted very quickly. She didn't wait…she called an ambulance immediately.'

Remembering the sadness in her mother's voice on the phone, she felt her throat swell. Her mother and Alistair had grown up together. They had known each other their whole lives. Before Oscar, Olivia had been engaged to Alistair. After she married Oscar, she and Alistair went back to being friends—better friends than she had ever managed to be with her husband.

'I don't know what she'll do if anything happens.'

'She's stronger than you think,' he said quietly.

There was that certainty again, and it hit her then with a jolt that Gabriel had spoken to her mother. Obviously, she knew that—she'd been there when they'd talked—but somehow the knowledge had got swallowed up and swept aside in all the panic. But after all this time it had happened, and she sensed that her mother had liked him, and that probably she would always have liked him. Only now it was too late to matter.

She took a deep, shaky breath. 'She's never been very good at fighting back.'

There were a few seconds of silence, and then Gabriel said quietly, 'You don't need to be a fighter to have strength. But whatever happens, we'll face it together.' His fingers tightened around hers. 'I'm not going anywhere.'

Her heart felt as if it was being squeezed in a vice.

It was the kind of thing people said in dramas on TV. It didn't mean anything. She tried not to think about how much she wanted it to mean something.

But there was no time to think about that anymore. They had arrived.

In the car, some of her panic had subsided. But now, breathing in the hospital smell of cleaning fluid and vending machine coffee, she felt it return. There were people everywhere. Sitting, shuffling, rushing... But somehow Gabriel seemed to know exactly which way to go, and she let him lead her through the corridors until finally they reached a pair of swing doors.

'Your mother's in there.' He gestured towards the doors. 'She's probably not had anything to eat or drink, so I'll go and see if I can find something.'

'Aren't you coming in with me?' She felt a rush of panic, although she wasn't sure if it was the thought of him leaving or the fact that the need in her was so close to the surface.

'Your mum will want to talk to you.' He put his arms around her, gathering her against him, and then gently pushed her away. 'I'll wait out here for you.'

His eyes were so very blue, like the sky above the island and the sea where the dolphins had ridden through the waves, and she felt a pang almost like homesickness as she pushed through the doors and walked into a waiting area.

'Dove!'

'Mum!'

'Oh, darling...'

Dove felt her face crumple as her mother stepped towards her and they hugged one another tightly. Olivia looked tired and pale, but she was still recognisably her mum.

'Have you seen him? Is he okay?' she asked.

Olivia nodded. 'They let me sit with him for about ten minutes. He's very weak, but he knew who I was, and he sent his love to you. He doesn't want you to worry.'

That was typical of Alistair. Even when he was lying in a hospital bed he was worrying about other people.

'Was it a stroke?'

Olivia shook her head. 'I thought it was, but it's something called sepsis.'

Dove felt her heartbeat punch upwards into her throat. 'What is that?'

For a moment her mother's face seemed to break up, but then she rallied. She *was* strong, Dove thought, just like Gabriel had said.

'I'm not really sure. They did try and explain, but I just couldn't take it in. I think it's when the body overreacts to an infection. Sit down, darling...' She guided Dove onto a chair.

'What kind of infection?' Dove asked as she sat down.

Olivia reached out and took her hands. 'Apparently he cut his foot the other week, when he was out in the garden, and it must have got infected. The nurse said that anyone can get sepsis, but apparently if you're diabetic you have trouble fighting it.'

'Is it dangerous?'

Olivia hesitated, then nodded. 'It can be. But he's responding to the antibiotics, and they've given him some other drugs, but I can't remember their names.'

Dove glanced across the waiting room. A nurse at the desk was talking to one of the porters. On the wall above their heads a clock was loudly ticking, marking the minutes. Nobody was wailing, and everything felt reassuringly calm, so she was able to say quite normally, 'He's going to get through this.'

'Yes, he is.' Her mother frowned and swallowed hard. 'He has to.'

Dove stared at her mother's bowed head. She looked as if she was praying. Or asking for forgiveness. And then, from nowhere, she remembered what Olivia had said earlier on the phone, about not being able to wake Alistair up.

Only why would her mother be waking him up?

Across the room the nurse was still talking, and the clock was still ticking, but inside her everything was still and silent, as if her heart had forgotten how to beat.

Her head was spinning, and old familiar shapes were turning around and upside down to form a new picture.

'You love him, don't you?' she said slowly. And as she spoke the words out loud it was like watching a film that seemed unfamiliar and then realising halfway through that you had seen it before and already knew the ending. 'You love Alistair—not just as a friend, I mean.'

There was a short silence, and then her mother nodded slowly, her eyes filling with tears. 'I'm so sorry, Dove. I should never have married your father. I knew it was a mistake almost immediately. We both did. But I was young and thoughtless and vain, and I didn't know the difference then between love and being in love. By the time I did it was too late. I know you must be shocked and angry and hurt and disappointed, and you have every right to be all of those things.'

Maybe she was a very strange person, Dove thought, searching inside herself, because she didn't feel any of those things. But maybe that was because Alistair was such a big part of their lives anyway. He was always there—helping, encouraging, listening...

'I'm not angry, Mum.' Reaching out, she took Olivia's hands. 'I suppose I'm confused. I don't understand why you and Dad stayed married.'

Her mother sighed. 'It's complicated.'

It was an echo of another conversation...with Gabriel. 'So simplify it, then,' she said softly. 'If you could sum up your reasons in three words, what would they be?'

There was a short silence. Olivia's face was strained and sad. 'I don't need three words,' she said, then hesitated, as if considering what she was about to say. 'I can do it in one,' she said finally. 'Blackmail.'

Dove stared at her mother. *Now* she was in shock. Around her, the walls of the waiting room seemed to be swaying.

'I don't… I don't understand.'

'Your father always needed money. My inheritance gave us a generous allowance, but he always needed more—only it was all tied up in a watertight trust for you and your sisters. Perhaps if he had joined his family's firm he would have known that,' Olivia said, and there was an exhaustion in her voice that cut through Dove's shock.

'So he found out about you and Alistair and blackmailed you?' Dove felt as if she was feeling her way in the dark, hands outstretched, each tentative step offering different, unknown choices. 'What did you do? Did you borrow money?'

Her mother was shaking her head. 'He did know about Alistair, but Oscar had multiple affairs, so he couldn't use that. He found out something else.' She bit her lip. 'Guessed, really. But it was enough.' She sounded very, very tired.

'What was enough?' Asking the question made Dove's back prickle. 'What did he guess?'

Olivia took a breath. Her shoulders were braced, as if for the impact of what she was about to say. 'That you weren't his daughter. That Alistair was your father.'

Later, Dove would wonder if she had always known. Now, though, she was just trying to pull her head together.

'Does Alistair know?' she asked.

Olivia nodded slowly, her eyes bright. 'I told him. And I told Oscar I was going to leave him.'

'But you didn't?'

Now she shook her head. 'Oscar went to see Alistair and threatened him. He said that he would go to court, make everything public and drag it out for as long as possible. Alistair was devastated. He felt so guilty—we both did—and he loved you girls.' Her face softened. 'Especially you.'

Dove swallowed past the lump in her throat. She could almost feel Alistair's love for her, vibrating in her mother's voice.

'So what happened?'

There was a brief silence, and she watched as her mother returned reluctantly to her story.

'Alistair told me that he didn't want to break up our marriage. And he agreed to subsidise Oscar's lifestyle. I only found that out after Oscar died that he left a mountain of debt that Alistair's been trying to clear for years. He's had to re-mortgage his house...the offices.' Her lip trembled 'I'm so sorry, Dove. None of this was meant to happen. One thing just led to another, and I was selfish and weak. I'm not expecting you to forgive me, because I don't deserve it—'

'There's nothing to forgive. We can't choose who we love.' Dove felt her heart contract. She was thinking not about Alistair, but Gabriel. She squeezed her mother's hands. 'Why now? Why did you decide to tell me all of this now?'

Olivia looked down at their hands. 'We've spent so much time not being the couple we could have been…the family we wanted to be. Seeing Alistair lying there, with all those tubes and wires, it felt like a sign for me to be brave. To stop living a half-life. Because life is shorter than you think. But it's also wonderful, too. Or it can be, if you let it.'

She was crying, and Dove was too, and suddenly they were clinging to one another.

Finally her mother let go of her. 'I know he wasn't a good person, but please don't think too harshly of Oscar. I don't think he knew how to love…but he did try. Strangely enough, he tried the hardest with you.'

They hugged again, for a long time. The clock ticked steadily above Dove's head, but she didn't hear it. She couldn't see the hands moving. All she could see was Gabriel's face…the curve of his jaw as he told the pilot to turn the plane around and the softness in his blue eyes as he pulled her into his arms.

She had thought it was too late for them, but her mother and Alistair had shown her that wasn't true.

She just had to be brave.

And find Gabriel.

The corridor was empty. Gabriel glanced at his watch. Probably some shift was changing, or maybe the hospital was always quieter after lunch. It was lucky he had only bought one coffee otherwise it would be cold by now. But the sandwiches and cold drinks should be good for a while.

His stomach clenched—not with hunger, but with an anxiety that seemed to be hotwired into all five senses. He could feel it vibrating through his body, taste it in his mouth, hear it in the jerkiness of his heartbeat. Watching Dove push through those doors, he had wanted to follow her, to shield her with his body against what lay on the other side, and it had taken every ounce of his willpower not to go with her.

Only he'd known that it wasn't right for him to be there. He wasn't family. He was an outsider...a stranger.

There was a sudden unbearable ache in his chest. If he hadn't let the past get in the way it might have been so different. But it *was* different now, he thought, remembering how he and Dove had talked, and how she could be quiet and listen too.

He felt a beat of hope, and let it take shape into something light and elliptical, like a piece of surf-smoothed volcanic rock from the beach at Pico. And he could be different. He could do that for her. He could forget about the acquisition. Write that letter to Fenella. Send it or not send it and get on with his life. *With Dove.*

The doors swung open and he felt his body loosen and tense at the same time as Dove stepped out of the waiting room, and then he was on his feet and pulling her against him, breathing in the light, clean scent of her as if it was pure oxygen.

They stayed like that for as long as he could justify it, and then he let her go. 'How's Alistair?'

'Tired and a bit shaken. It wasn't a stroke—he has sepsis. But they think they've caught it in time.' She smiled weakly. 'He's loving having all the nurses fussing all over him.'

His hand tightened around hers. 'Thank goodness.'

There was a luminous quality to her skin that seemed to light up the dingy corridor. She looked young and alive, almost eager.

'You care about him too?'

'Of course.' He spoke automatically, but it was true. He did care about Alistair. But why did that matter to Dove? 'So what happens now?' he asked.

'They said that he's got to stay in hospital for a couple of weeks, but everyone is really pleased with the progress he's made.'

She was watching him, waiting…

'But that's not all?' he said slowly.

There was a silence, and then she shook her head. 'My mum has just told me something. About Alistair.'

She met his gaze, and suddenly, looking down into her soft grey eyes, he knew what she was going to say.

'He's your father.'

His hands tightened around her waist as she stared up at him dazedly. 'How did you know that?'

'I didn't. But you have his eyes,' he said simply.

She blinked, then nodded. 'They love each other. They always have. And one night they gave in to their feelings. And...'

'And they still love each other?'

She nodded as he finished her sentence. 'They both feel as though they've waited so long to be together.'

There was another silence. 'Are you okay?' he asked finally.

She nodded. 'It's a lot to take in, but it makes sense of so much. And it feels right. It feels good. I feel like we can be a family.'

He could hear the hope in her voice, and he knew that she was remembering that photo of his family, picturing something once so out of reach, now there for the taking.

'There are other things too... They can wait, though. Everything else can wait. You see, there's something I have to tell you. Something I need to tell you. Something I realised when my mum was talking about love and obstacles and having to fight to get back to where you want to be.'

Her eyes were so open and soft it almost blinded him.

'I love you,' she said. 'I always have. I didn't want to for so long, but I couldn't not. And I think you love me too.'

Gabriel stared at her, holding his breath. She loved him. And he loved her. There was nothing to stop him. He looked down at her beautiful, hopeful face, seeing the sweetness of her, and the goodness. And now she was whole too. But he had nothing to give her. Nothing good—not like his father or Alistair.

But she wants you.

It was like saying a prayer or a poem. And for a moment he hesitated. He could take her hand and let her love him. There was nothing to stop him.

So he would have to stop himself.

Because if he took her hand, and her love, he might ruin her life.

Because he didn't know how to be whole. He didn't know if he could ever be whole, and not knowing for sure meant that he couldn't be with her.

He couldn't take the risk and maybe hurt her again. Hurt her more. He would do anything to make sure that didn't happen. Even give up the chance to be with her.

She was waiting for him to speak, and he needed to say something quickly, before he gave in to his need to be loved by this marvel of a woman.

'I'm sorry.' He lifted his hands from her waist carefully. 'I don't feel the same way,' he lied. 'I don't love you. Back on the island it felt brutal, just ending things between us, but I thought I'd made it clear that this was only ever a temporary arrangement.'

It hurt so much, watching her face change, and

he knew then that she did love him. Because she couldn't hide her confusion and her pain.

'But we were going to New York—'

'For fun.' He frowned. 'Look, I'm sorry if you got the wrong idea—'

'So what was all this for?'

She took a step towards him, and he knew what it must have cost her to do it, because he knew what it cost him to stop himself doing the same.

'You and me on the yacht and the island? Going to New York? Coming with me to London?'

Her gaze was steady, and she looked so serious, so determined, he felt like a child. And he *was* a child— a damaged child—and she deserved so much better.

Forcing himself to meet her eyes, he frowned again. 'We were on my plane and we were in mid-air. I had no choice but to come with you. The rest of it was just sex,' he lied again. 'But I won't deny that I still want you, so if you want to keep things casual then we can hook up when I'm in town, but as for anything else...'

He remembered her confronting him on the deck of *The Argentum* and he hated himself. But he couldn't be who she needed him to be. Not for certain. And not sure wasn't enough.

'I'm sorry,' he said again—and he was.

But he needed to put her off, keep her at arm's length, because if he touched her, felt the beat of her heart, then he wouldn't be strong enough to push her away.

'I know you don't want to hear this, but all I care about is getting this acquisition over the line. You were there, and we had some fun. But all this was about putting the past behind me. All of the past. Including you.'

The lie felt seismic. He could feel it expanding in every direction, so that he half thought the walls would start to crumble and fall.

And he wanted to be crushed.

Anything would be better than seeing Dove's eyes.

For one terrible moment he thought she might tell him she loved him again, but instead, in a voice that tore at him inside, she said quietly, 'I thought you were a good man. But you're not. You're just anger and emptiness all wrapped up in a beautiful skin.'

He forced himself to meet her eyes. 'You'll get over it.'

She stared at him in silence, her face small and pale and stunned, and then she turned and pushed through the doors.

He had known it would be like this, but it was still unbearable. He stared after her for a moment, telling himself that it had been the right thing to do, and that he'd done it for her, and then he too turned and walked away.

CHAPTER TEN

IN THE BOARDROOM of the Silva Group's headquarters in New York, Gabriel shifted back in his seat and gazed across the city skyline. It was eleven o'clock and the meeting had just broken up for coffee and the protein bars that were delivered every day by a local bakery.

But, unlike everyone else in the room, he wasn't interested in either. Nor was it eleven o'clock. For him, there was only one time. London time.

Picking up his phone, he turned it over in his hand.

It had been that way since the moment he'd returned to the States a month ago. At first he'd thought it was jet-lag. But then it had carried on, day after day, week after week. And now it was the fourth week, and it was just how he lived, mentally adding five hours on to the time that everyone else worked by.

Because despite the very real truth of his being here, in New York, his head and his heart had never left that hospital corridor in London.

He saw her face everywhere. Pale, devastated, crushed. And it hurt more than anything in his life. He wanted to put that part of himself away somewhere, so that he could forget her, but that would mean not seeing her face, and living was hard enough right now. He couldn't live in a world where he couldn't see Dove's face.

He missed her unbearably. It was continuous—an overwhelming, endless awareness of her absence.

And he didn't understand it. Every hour that passed should be easing his pain, but if anything it was getting worse. So many times he had almost picked up the phone and called her...

'Gabriel?'

He turned. His CFO Bill Brady was looking at him expectantly.

'Sorry...' He frowned. 'I was miles away.' *Three thousand four hundred and fifty-nine miles, to be precise.* 'Where are we at?'

'The acquisition.'

He stared at Bill blankly. What acquisition? The question echoed inside his head. And then he remembered, and he was stunned. How could he have forgotten? How could something that had been his purpose in life for so long suddenly be so unimportant?

His CFO cleared his throat. 'The Fairlight Holdings acquisition.'

Bill smiled at him, the kind of reassuring, placating smile you might use with someone who was lost.

And he *was* lost, Gabriel thought, his fingers tightening around the phone. Lost for so many years... held in limbo between an unknown past and a present that should be enough but always felt incomplete, so that his whole life he'd felt as if he was missing something.

Except with Dove.

With her, he wasn't lost in himself, or in the pull of the past. He was present and whole and happy.

'There's still some pushback about the name-change.' Bill was speaking in that same, careful way. 'But I think they're tiring. So we'll stand firm. Unless, of course, you've changed your mind?'

He felt the combined stares of the ten people sitting round the boardroom table. He thought about Dove, and he could hear her voice telling him that things were different...that *he* was different.

Still holding his phone, he shifted back in his seat. 'No, nothing's changed.'

It was a hot day in London.

Too hot, Dove thought, to be dragging boxes around. But luckily she was going to have help. Having made a proper nuisance of herself, her mother had managed to persuade the removal company to turn up a day early.

Although she didn't really mind wrapping up her mother's teacups and saucers in old newspapers, Dove thought. There was something oddly comforting about it, and it gave her a chance to think. Not brood. That would be a bad idea. But so was ignoring things, burying them, pretending they didn't exist.

It was hard to change her ways. It was what she had done all her life.

But not this time.

This time she was trying something different. Being someone different.

And that meant thinking about her father and Gabriel.

She had forgiven her father—and she still thought of him as that. She accepted that she would probably never know why he had done what he had to Gabriel, but she believed her mother when she said that Oscar had loved her.

Just as she'd believed Gabriel when he'd said that he didn't. Not in the way she needed and wanted him to love her.

She hadn't wanted to believe it…

Her chest folded in on itself as she remembered that terrible conversation at the hospital four weeks ago, and Gabriel's quiet but adamantine assertion.

'All this is about putting the past behind me. All of the past. Including you.'

He could have hardly made it clearer, and yet even as she'd walked back towards her mother she had hoped he might follow her, grab her arm and spin her around, tell her that he didn't mean it, that he was just scared, that he loved her…

Only he had done none of those things.

He had left her, just as he had six years ago. Only

this time there was no mix-up, no interference. He had gone because he'd wanted to go. Because she wasn't a reason to stay. She had made a fool of herself for nothing.

And yet she was glad she'd done it. It had been the right thing to do even if it had been the wrong man to do it for.

Her throat tightened momentarily. That was progress, at least. But then she wasn't alone this time.

Instead of hiding her pain, trying to cope, pretending that she was all right, she had walked straight back into that waiting room and burst into tears. She had cried for a long time, and then it had taken even longer to tell her mother everything.

Her mother had been amazing.

She had listened and comforted her, and then she had called the Silva Group in London and told them that her daughter was taking compassionate leave.

So now Dove was at home, organising her mother's house move. At first she had been worried that she wouldn't have enough to do, but every morning her mother handed her a list written in her neat, copperplate writing and she worked her way through it.

Most of the tasks required nothing more than a phone and a fair amount of determination, but everything took a surprising amount of time and effort, and the days had turned into weeks.

It was hard, getting used to Gabriel not being there in her heart, but one of these days she knew she would wake up from a Gabriel-free sleep and not think of him. It wouldn't always feel as if she'd had open heart surgery without an anaesthetic. Like he'd said, she would get over it—get over him.

In the meantime, there were other things—good things—to take the edge off the pain. Now that she was off the acquisition there was her job, and there was this new and entirely astonishingly effortless version of her family—and, best of all, Alistair was coming home this afternoon.

Alistair had recovered well. He was still tired, but he couldn't seem to stop smiling, and it was a joy to watch him and her mother laughing and teasing one another about their upcoming wedding. Their easy love for one another was building on her newfound faith in relationships, and she no longer imagined marriage as a trap or a cage. Rather, she could see how it could be a partnership, with boundaries, but also room to grow and be your best self.

She cut the packing tape and yanked it over the bulging box, and then sat on it quickly as it threatened to burst open.

Now that they were together officially there was no need for Olivia and Alistair to have a house each. Dove glanced around the kitchen, with its surfeit of cooking implements and spice jars. She had no idea how they were going to fit all of this in one house, though. But they would work it out, she thought, and it was a good feeling being able to think that.

She heard the doorbell ring and felt a rush of relief. *Now, where was that list?*

Sticking her head through the open window, she shouted up to the man who was presumably joined to the pair of trainers she could see on the doorstep.

'It's open,' she called up. 'Just let yourself in. I'm downstairs.'

She heard the door open, then close, and footsteps on the staircase.

'Thanks for fitting us in today. I thought we'd start in the bedroom, if that's all right with you?'

'The bedroom sounds perfect.'

Her heartbeat faltered. Her mouth seemed to lose its shape and she felt her legs sway beneath her.

Gabriel was standing in the kitchen. Against her mother's pastel pink saucepans and delicate floral blinds and tablecloth he looked too big, too male, and she edged to the other side of the table as memories of facing him across another table jostled with her heartbeat for space inside her head. It was only six weeks ago, but it felt like a lifetime.

'What are you doing here?'

For a moment he didn't reply, and then he said quite calmly, as if he was in the habit of turning up in her mother's kitchen unannounced, 'I need to talk to you about the acquisition.'

She stared at him in disbelief, feeling the blood rushing to her head, and a kind of mindless anger that had no name swelling inside her. Was he insane? Did he actually think he could just walk in here and start talking to her about acquisitions after everything that had happened?

'Firstly, I'm off work,' she told him. 'On compassionate leave—not that I'd expect you to understand the concept of compassion. Secondly, I don't want to talk to you about anything. So I suggest you go back up the stairs you just came down. Oh, and shut the door on your way out,' she added.

He didn't move.

Obviously. Because he was delusional or utterly without empathy, or both.

'You have ten seconds to get out of this house.' She picked up her phone. 'And then I'm calling the police.'

Gabriel stared at the woman he loved, his heart beating like a drum in his chest. Walking up to the house, he'd felt more like himself, and hopeful. Now, though, he could feel his hope draining away.

Dove was furious. Beneath her obvious confusion and shock at having him turn up at her mother's home he could see her frustration in the clean, curving lines of her face and the storm clouds of her eyes, and he couldn't blame her. But nor could he do what she had told him to do.

'I will leave. But first you need to listen to what I have to say.'

She was staring at him as if he was mad. And maybe he was. His team certainly thought so. In his mind he replayed the meeting two days ago, when Bill Brady had asked him about the Fairlight acquisition. For so long it had been his goal, but sitting

there in the boardroom it had suddenly seemed distant and irrelevant to him, almost as if it was happening to someone else. He had felt the way he had
back in that hotel with Charles Lambton, when he
had felt like a stranger to himself.

Only that hadn't been supposed to happen. He
had wanted to buy out Fairlight Holdings so he could
erase Fenella's family business, as she had erased
him, but suddenly he had felt as if he was erasing
himself.

To the complete astonishment of the men and
women sitting round the table, he had got to his feet
and cut short the meeting, striding out of the office
without so much as one word of explanation.

'Or else what?' Dove's grey eyes narrowed on
his face. 'What are you going to do? Threaten me?
Threaten my family.'

'No, but I won't leave until you've heard me out.
And you know me well enough to believe me when
I say that.'

Dove glared at him. She should call the police, but
the last thing Alistair needed was to come home to
yet more flashing blue lights.

'Fine. You have five minutes—starting now.' She
lifted her chin. 'But I don't know why you're both-
ering. I'm not going to be working on the acquisition anymore.'

'No, you're not,' he said quietly. 'Because there
isn't going to be one.'

She stared at him in confusion, her heart tight inside her chest, feeling worried despite herself. She knew how badly Gabriel had wanted the acquisition to happen.

'What happened? Was it the name-change? Did they pull out?'

There was silence.

'No, I did. I went to see Fenella, like you suggested.'

He had? Her head was spinning like a Waltzer. Why had he done that? More importantly, what had Fenella said?

'How was it?' she asked, choosing her words with care.

He tilted his head back and, seeing the strain around his eyes, she had to stop herself from reaching out and taking his hand. It wasn't hers to take, she reminded herself. And yet it hurt to leave him standing there alone.

'She was upset. Then angry. And then upset again.' He let out a breath. 'It didn't change anything between us.'

'I'm sorry.' She meant it. Even though he had hurt her, she didn't want him to be hurt.

He shook his head. 'Don't be. It wasn't easy, or enjoyable, but I'm glad I did it. It changed how I feel about her. Filled in a few fairly crucial gaps.'

There was a silence, and then he said quietly, 'It made me realise that my birth mother and father might have given me my genes, but my adoptive parents and my family gave me my identity. And I would never have worked that out without you.'

His blue eyes rested on her face, not blazing with anger or hurt any more, but light and calm.

'I wanted to thank you for making me see things differently.'

'You came all the way from New York to thank me?'

She stared at him in bewilderment, her earlier anger fading and morphing into something more dangerous.

Why did he have to go and do that?

For weeks now she had been telling herself that he was a monster, without a soul or a conscience, but now he was here in her mother's kitchen, apologising, looking young and serious and contrite, and making her feel things, want things…

'I have business in London.' He shrugged. 'A couple of new acquisitions.'

Of course he did, She swallowed, her skin tightening at her own stupidity. 'Well, don't let me stop you.'

He took a step closer. 'But that's the thing—you *have* stopped me. I can't do anything. I can't sleep. I'm not eating. My staff think I've lost my mind… What I'm trying to say is that I made a mistake.'

The strain in his voice made her stomach clench painfully, so that she had to grip the edge of the table to stop herself doubling up.

'We both made mistakes,' she said.

'I should never have left you in the hospital.'

It's guilt, that's all, she told herself. And that was a good thing. Because it meant that deep down he cared about things, and she was glad for him. Only it wasn't fair that she should find that out now, when she was trying so hard not to care about him.

She shook her head. 'You can't do this, Gabriel. You can't come here and say things like that to me. It's not fair—'

He took another step closer, and the blue of his eyes was like the sea and the sky, so that looking into them was like drowning and flying both together.

'It's love,' he said hoarsely. 'And everything's fair in love and war, Dove. Only I think we've done the war bit, don't you?'

Her heart was beating in her throat, so that it was hard to swallow, to speak, and she couldn't breathe past her hope and longing.

'But you don't love me.'

'But I do.'

His face shifted, his expression suddenly so sweet and sure and steady that she couldn't stop a sob from leaving her throat.

'I love you, and I need you, and I know I made a mess of things, and that it's probably too late, but I had to tell you. That's why I came to London.'

He reached over and took her hands in his.

'To tell you that you were right. I *am* different—because you changed me. I thought that punishing my mother, taking something from her, would make me feel whole, but it's you who makes me feel whole.'

His fingers tightened slightly. 'You remember when I told you I was angry? I was. All the time. Raging deep down. But I'm not angry anymore. And that's because of you. Because you're a good person. The way you see things makes them better. You've made me better.'

His expression, with all its need and hope, went straight into her, filling her like sunlight.

'You're a good person too,' she said shakily.

Her hands were shaking too now, and Gabriel reached out and pulled her close, not kissing her, just holding her, slotting her body into his like a key in a lock.

'I'm sorry… I'm sorry,' he whispered into her soft clean hair. 'For what I said…for what I did…'

'I know.'

And now they kissed, soft and gentle at first, and then with heat and longing and love. So much love it seemed to fill the kitchen with sunlight.

'How did you know I was here?'

'I spoke to your mother.' He grimaced. 'She sounds like a debutante on the phone, but she was surprisingly fierce in person.'

'You've met my mother?' Dove's mouth dropped open. 'When?'

'Yesterday.'

His arms tightened around her, his gaze reaching inside her, warming her, caressing her.

'I wanted to talk to her first. About you. About

us. I didn't want there to be any confusion. Or any secrets.' He hesitated. 'And then I spoke to Alistair.'

A great tangle of emotion was swirling inside her. 'You went to see him at the hospital?'

He nodded slowly. 'I needed to talk to him about the acquisitions. Actually, one of them is more of a merger.'

She felt his hands slide down to her hips, holding her gently but firmly.

'A very specific merger,' he said softly. 'The only merger that matters to me.'

He reached into his pocket and pulled out a small square box, his eyes blazing not with anger but with something that burned inside her too.

'Marry me, Dove. You have my heart. You are my life. Let me love you and care for you.'

Tears sliding down her cheeks, she nodded, and he slid the ring onto her finger and they kissed again. Some time later they broke apart, but they stayed close, their hands moving over one another in relief and wonder, as if neither of them could quite believe that they were there, together.

'You said there was an acquisition too.' Dove frowned. 'What is it?'

She watched his face change, tense a little.

'Cavendish and Cox.'

For a moment she didn't react, and Gabriel waited, his heart accelerating a little.

'And Alistair knows about this?'

He nodded, curving his hands round her body, anchoring her against him.

'Your mother told me what Oscar did.' He hesitated. 'And I know the sepsis could have happened to anybody, but Alistair's been pushing himself for years. This way he can slow down a little. Enjoy life with his new family.'

He felt her arms slide up around his neck. 'I said you were a good person.'

He smiled then, and she felt her whole body open up to him like a flower to the sun.

'Well, to be absolutely truthful, I have been looking into acquiring a law firm for a couple of years now, and it just so happens my fiancée works for one.'

Gabriel felt a jolt of astonishment and elation as he used the word, and the rightness of everything blossomed inside him.

'So you're going to buy us out?'

He shook his head. 'I'd invest in the business. But I would be more of a sleeping partner.'

She leaned into him, her heart somersaulting. 'I'm not sure that would work. I don't remember you doing much sleeping.'

His blue eyes were steady on her face, and there was a softness in them that she couldn't turn away from. With joy, she realised that she didn't have to, not now—or ever.

'That reminds me—didn't you say something about starting in the bedroom?' he said softly.

And then he laughed, and she laughed too, and then they were kissing as if the world was ending… but for them it was only just beginning.

* * * * *

#4097 A BABY TO MAKE HER HIS BRIDE
Four Weddings and a Baby
by Dani Collins
One night is all Jasper can offer Vienna. The people closest to him always get hurt. But when Jasper learns Vienna is carrying his baby, he must take things one step further to protect them both... with his diamond ring!

#4098 EXPECTING HER ENEMY'S HEIR
A Billion-Dollar Revenge
by Pippa Roscoe
Alessandro stole Amelia's birthright—and she intends to prove it! Even if that means working undercover at the Italian billionaire's company... But their off-limits attraction brings her revenge plan crashing down when she discovers that she's carrying Alessandro's baby!

#4099 THE ITALIAN'S INNOCENT CINDERELLA
by Cathy Williams
When shy Maude needs a last-minute plus-one, she strikes a deal with the one man she trusts—her boss! But claiming to date ultrarich Mateo drags Maude's name into the headlines... And now she must make convenient vows with the Italian!

#4100 VIRGIN'S NIGHT WITH THE GREEK
Heirs to a Greek Empire
by Lucy King
Artist Willow's latest high-society portrait is set to make her career. Until the subject's son, Leonidas, demands it never see the light of day! He's everything she isn't. Yet their negotiations can't halt her red-hot reaction to the Greek...

HPCNMRA0323

#4101 BOUND BY A SICILIAN SECRET
by Lela May Wight

Flora strayed from her carefully scripted life and lost herself in the kisses of a Sicilian stranger. Overwhelmed, she fled his bed and returned to her risk-free existence. Now Raffaele has found her, and together they discover the unimaginable—she's pregnant!

#4102 STOLEN FOR HIS DESERT THRONE
by Heidi Rice

After finding raw passion with innocent—and headstrong—Princess Kaliah, desert Prince Kamal feels honor-bound to offer marriage. But that's the last thing independent Liah wants! His solution? Stealing her away to his oasis to make her see reason!

#4103 THE HOUSEKEEPER AND THE BROODING BILLIONAIRE
by Annie West

Since his tragic loss, Alessio runs his empire from his secluded Italian *castello*. Until his new housekeeper, Charlotte, opens his eyes to the world he's been missing. But can he maintain his impenetrable emotional walls once their powerful chemistry is unleashed?

#4104 HIRED FOR HIS ROYAL REVENGE
Secrets of the Kalyva Crown
by Lorraine Hall

AI is hired to help Greek billionaire Lysias avenge his parents' murders...by posing as a long-lost royal *and* his fiancée! But when an unruly spark flares between them, she can't shake the feeling that she *belongs* by his side...

YOU CAN FIND MORE INFORMATION ON UPCOMING HARLEQUIN TITLES, FREE EXCERPTS AND MORE AT HARLEQUIN.COM.

HPCNMRB0323

Get 4 FREE REWARDS!

We'll send you 2 FREE Books plus 2 FREE Mystery Gifts.

FREE Value Over **$20**

Both the **Harlequin® Desire** and **Harlequin Presents®** series feature compelling novels filled with passion, sensuality and intriguing scandals.

YES! Please send me 2 FREE novels from the Harlequin Desire or Harlequin Presents series and my 2 FREE gifts (gifts are worth about $10 retail). After receiving them, if I don't wish to receive any more books, I can return the shipping statement marked "cancel." If I don't cancel, I will receive 6 brand-new Harlequin Presents Larger-Print books every month and be billed just $6.30 each in the U.S. or $6.49 each in Canada, a savings of at least 10% off the cover price, or 6 Harlequin Desire books every month and be billed just $5.05 each in the U.S. or $5.74 each in Canada, a savings of at least 12% off the cover price. It's quite a bargain! Shipping and handling is just 50¢ per book in the U.S. and $1.25 per book in Canada.* I understand that accepting the 2 free books and gifts places me under no obligation to buy anything. I can always return a shipment and cancel at any time by calling the number below. The free books and gifts are mine to keep no matter what I decide.

Choose one: ☐ **Harlequin Desire**
(225/326 HDN GRJ7)

☐ **Harlequin Presents Larger-Print**
(176/376 HDN GRJ7)

Name (please print)

Address _____ Apt. #

City _____ State/Province _____ Zip/Postal Code

Email: Please check this box ☐ if you would like to receive newsletters and promotional emails from Harlequin Enterprises ULC and its affiliates. You can unsubscribe anytime.

Mail to the Harlequin Reader Service:
IN U.S.A.: P.O. Box 1341, Buffalo, NY 14240-8531
IN CANADA: P.O. Box 603, Fort Erie, Ontario L2A 5X3

Want to try 2 free books from another series! Call 1-800-873-8635 or visit www.ReaderService.com.

HARLEQUIN
PLUS

Try the best multimedia subscription service for romance readers like you!

Read, Watch and Play.

Experience the easiest way to get the romance content you crave.

Start your **FREE TRIAL** at
<u>www.harlequinplus.com/freetrial</u>.